Bunny

and the

Bear

Furry United Coalition #1

Eve Langlais

New York Times Bestseller

Copyright © July 2011, Eve Langlais
Cover Art by Amanda Kelsey © July 2011
Edited by Victoria Miller
Edited by Devin Govaere
Line Edited Brieanna Roberston

Produced in Canada

Published by Eve Langlais
1606 Main Street, PO Box 151,
Stittsville, Ontario, Canada, K2S1A3

www.EveLanglais.com

ISBN-13: 978-1534914421
ISBN-10: 1534914420

Bunny And The Bear is a work of fiction and the characters, events and dialogue found within the story are of the author's imagination and are not to be construed as real. Any resemblance to actual events or persons, either living or deceased, is completely coincidental.

Prologue

Thirty years ago…

Bottom of the food chain indeed. Fuming in the corner of the schoolyard didn't make the words any easier to swallow. *I just wanted a turn playing too. Bullies.*

Glaring at them didn't retract their cruel taunts. *They didn't need to call me shrimp, or pipsqueak, and the munchkin song they sang in chorus was totally uncalled for.*

Did the rats with their beady eyes garner this kind of disrespect? The sly foxes or the ditzy bunnies? Well, actually, the bunnies did—stupid, long-eared, lettuce eaters.

Father shared a good portion of the blame, that fidgety squirrel with a few missing screws. Why was it everyone else had parents who belonged to some really cool and large animal caste? Or at least something with great big claws? Inheriting the genes of a pair of weaklings sucked, as did the diminutive size that restricted game participation. "You wouldn't be able to hold your own," they scoffed, and the even more mortifying, "Hey, we've got a position for you…as the ball." Judging a person by their physical attributes and inner animal was so unfair.

And I hate unfair.

So what could a poor, unappreciated, puny-sized

tween with an overdeveloped brain do?

Eyeing the larger children on the schoolyard, a plan formed. As the other children played their rough games and flaunted their prowess, serious plotting occurred—interspersed with the need to push up wide-framed glasses, another genetic anomaly not common to shape shifters to place at the feet of parents who should have never procreated. Once the basic outline for revenge emerged, an evil laugh slipped out. Actually, it sounded more like a sputtering choke, but there was plenty of time to improve the menacing chuckle of success because it took almost twenty years to put the plan in motion. *But when the time comes, I'll make them all pay.*

Muaha—urgh—muaha—cough.

Chapter One

Talk about hypnotic—and cock hardening. The bouncing little ass, which he almost bumped into—at just the right height—bobbed from side to side right outside his apartment door. The owner of the delectable bottom, bent over out of sight, hummed as she gyrated. Indecent shorts covered her creamy globes, but barely. Her apparel appeared at least a size too small given the amount of cheek peeking from the ragged hems. Hell, in her current position, he could even tell she shaved, a fact his dick approved of, which of course irritated him to no end.

Chase didn't know whether he should slap the round buttocks to get the female's attention or growl at her to get out of the way. Curbing his third urge, which involved grinding himself against the inviting bottom— preferably naked—he cleared his throat. "Ahem."

Silky platinum, almost white hair flew up to slap him in the face as the woman straightened. The skein of hair caught on the bristles of his jaw, and he shook his head with a grumble as he spat out the strand that got in his mouth. A whiff of her shampoo, an intoxicating raspberry scent, made his tummy rumble, but not in hunger, unless carnal counted.

With a twirl, the flexing female faced him with a full-lipped smile that seemed much too cheerful this time of the morning.

"Well, hello there, neighbor," she chirped, her brightness so sweet he ached for his toothbrush. "Sorry I'm in the way. I was just warming up for my morning jog. I don't think we've met. I just moved in to apartment 9C." She thrust her hand out and twitched her nose at him as she continued to beam.

Chase scowled as he ignored her outstretched hand. One whiff and he could tell she didn't belong to the human genome. Damned bunnies and their sunny natures. How could he properly rebuke her with her grinning like the world's cutest simpleton? A guy bunny he could have cuffed upside the head, but a girl one... Somehow, he didn't think gagging her with his cock was the way to chastise her. "So you were the reason why I didn't get to sleep in on Saturday? Could your moving guys have been any louder?"

Her vivid green eyes blinked, her lips lost their lilt, and he noticed a smattering of freckles across the bridge of her nose. "But it was eleven o'clock in the morning. The landlord assured me it would be fine. Did you go to bed late?"

He fixed a glare on her and replied in a haughty tone, "I like at least a good sixteen hours on the weekend, eighteen even sometimes. Because of your ruckus, though, I only got a measly fourteen." With winter only slowly losing its grip on the city, the urge to hibernate in his bed remained hard to shake.

"Hmm, last time I spent that long in bed, it wasn't because I was sleeping," she sassed with a wink.

The innuendo was impossible to miss, and while an insane urge to drag her back to his bedroom and test his bed's springs did cross his mind, he instead feigned ignorance and frowned. "Then you should get a better mattress. Sleep should never be neglected." He fixed her with a hard stare. "Or interrupted."

A grin curled her lips and displayed gleaming white teeth. "Aww, aren't you the most adorable grumpy bear. Tell you what. I'll make it up to you. Let me fix you some dinner."

Hmm, naked wet bunny on a plate? "No," he growled.

"Freshly baked chocolate chip cookies?"

No, but he knew a sweet pastry he'd like to taste. *Damn.* His mind refused to get out of the gutter this morning. "No."

Her nose twitched. "Massage?"

Greasy hands sliding all over his body and over his dick. Yeah, that sounded like a plan. *Hunh, wait a second.* "No." Chase needed to leave before the hard-on in his pants tore through the fabric and went after the little bunny's pie, but she stood squarely in front of him, looking and smelling much too yummy.

Not at all perturbed by his negative replies, the luscious female rabbit tapped her chin with a finger as her eyes, narrowed in thought, held his gaze. He stared right back, trying to appear ferocious. She didn't seem to notice. Cocking her head to the side, she eyed him up and down. Despite himself, he sucked his stomach in, bulking up his already massive chest. A bear did have his pride after all.

"I think I'll just surprise you," she said with a wink and a lick of her lips.

His cock jerked as Chase almost went cross-eyed at the thought of what she might do—naked. "Please don't," he grumbled. Too late. The bunny, whose name he'd never gotten, sprinted off, her silken hair bouncing down her back, drawing attention to the exposed round cheeks of ass, her slap-me, bite-me, plow-me, perfect ass.

A long-suffering sigh escaped him. *I must really need to get laid if even small woodland creatures are turning me on.*

Adjusting his dick, which refused to play dead, Chase grabbed his briefcase and headed off to work. A brisk walk would help clear his mind.

One of the advantages of city living was he rented an office within blocks of his apartment, right across the street from a bakery that sold the most delicious honey buns. Were the two items related? Kind of. He'd noticed the Office for Rent sign while chowing down on some of the pastries. Setting up an office right across the street from his favorite bakery seemed like fate to a bear who couldn't get enough sweets. He blamed his mother, who, once he'd graduated from university, moved to the mountains, taking her delicious dessert-making skills with her. Chase, while an accomplished chef when it came to meat and potato dishes, sucked at making the more delicate confections he craved. Thank Ursa for bakeries.

Thinking of the sticky buns—soft and chewy, their glazed sugar melting on his tongue—made him hungry, so he grabbed a dozen and ordered another two dozen for a later pickup before heading up the elevator to his office. Entering his space on the third floor, he greeted Katy, his receptionist, a she-wolf who managed to be ultra-efficient without ever seeming to work. An admirable trait, if you asked him.

She currently filed her immaculate nails. "Your

inbox has some contracts needing your final look-over and signature. You have a will probate at eleven. And another at three." On and on, she recited the tasks she'd undertaken and passed on to him for completion. Boring. His punishment, he guessed, for taking the easier path to will and probate attorney instead of criminal.

"Why can't you be a lazy-ass secretary like everybody else's?" he grumbled as his day began to look more and more bleak.

"Just making sure you've got money for my summer bonus," she replied. "Which reminds me…"

Before she could go off on another list, the phone rang and, with a sigh of relief, Chase escaped.

The first thing he did when he sat behind his large wooden desk was scarf down three pastries. His sweet tooth assuaged, he still found himself hungry, just not for food. The damned bunny still bounced around inside his mind and had him raring for a taste of pie, and not just any pie, her sweet pie.

It baffled him—*I don't even like cute and perky women.* It annoyed him—*Since when do I lust after anything but a sow?* Attempts to change the direction of his thoughts failed, and after fifteen minutes of restless fidgeting and busy work, he came to the conclusion that nothing would curb his arousal but sex itself. *Not with that bloody cheerful rabbit, though.*

Pulling out his cell phone, Chase scrolled through the numbers, looking for a lady-friend to call—AKA a fuck buddy. None of the names appealed to him, and despite himself, he couldn't stop picturing the cute little bunny and her full pink lips, perfect for sucking dick. He clearly recalled her large, plush breasts straining at her snug T-shirt, a hefty handful made for grabbing and squeezing—and burying his face between to blow raspberries. Then there was her indented waist, just the right size for his hands to hoist her sweet little body up and indulge in some hardcore plowing. *I bet she's a screamer.* And what about her full hips, made for bearing cubs?

Whoa. Chase almost fell out of his office chair at the last thought. *How did I go from getting rid of a hard-on to babies?* Settling down wasn't part of any current plan, especially not with a bunny. Interspecies mating was all well and good for other shifters. As the firstborn son descended of pureblood bears, he owed it to his ancestors to keep their line untainted. Let his brother, Mason, the ladies man of the family, break tradition.

When I'm ready for cubs, I'll settle down with a nice sow with good genes—and a fat ass for slapping. Maybe I'll find myself a feisty Kodiak or a polar female, but nothing crazier than that. As a grizzly, he did have a reputation to maintain, after all.

As for his long-eared neighbor and her threat to make it up to him, he'd just work harder at being his usual charming self. It scared off most everybody—human or shifter—eventually. *And that's how I like it. Friends and lovers expect things of you, like a helping hand, or sharing the blankets when you're in the same bed, or splitting your dessert when there's only one honey cruller left.* His last girlfriend had been big on the whole share-everything scenario. It was why their relationship never made it past the three-month mark because, after all, why split anything when he could just keep it all for himself?

Of course, his current course of keeping his cock

to himself wasn't working out as well, apparently. Not only was his hand tired of fisting, nothing could compare to the tight, hot feel of a…platinum blonde bouncing on it with energetic yells.

The phone rang, and his bunny-caused erection wilted at the shrill voice of Mrs. Plantain.

****

Miranda alternately jogged and sprinted all sixteen blocks to work, not bothering to take notice of or respond to the catcalls and honking horns that followed her wherever she went. In a great mood, she smiled as she traveled and only caused one fender bender when she paused to bend over to pick up a lucky penny. There were no casualties, proving the tarnished copper cent was worth it. *It's my lucky day.*

She'd just met the most entertaining male. *Don't forget sexy too.* Towering over her at six and a half feet, the man was built like a brick house—solid muscle without an ounce of fat, so yummy. Dressed in a suit, with an honest-to-goodness knotted tie instead of a clip-on, he appeared so staid and proper. It made a bunny want to do crazy things to see if she could get him to crack a smile. But talk about grim. She'd never seen such a dour countenance on anyone, and him still so young too. She pegged him at probably only a few years older than her twenty-seven. *Betcha I could turn that frown upside down.* If he gave her a chance before throttling her. He didn't seem like a guy who owned loads of patience or people skills.

However, despite his unpleasant demeanor, she found him intriguing. He roused her curious bunny nature because now she wanted to know what made him so rude and what it would take for him to laugh—or grab her in a bear hug for a seriously hot smooch.

Entering a nondescript office building, Miranda hopped into an open elevator and pressed thirteen. As the cab moved, she ignored the interested looks of the humans. Males of any species were so easy to distract. Just throw on a pair of Daisy Dukes and a tight T, and they turned into drooling idiots. They were so cute sometimes.

Unable to keep still, she rolled back and forth on her heels as the elevator went up and up, disgorging humans as it went. At the final floor, it dinged, but before the doors opened, a tingling sensation swept her as a security laser checked her to make sure she belonged on this level. Ascertaining her shifter status, the doors slid open, and she bounced out into the vestibule for FUC—Furry United Coalition. Originally, they were called Furry United Coalition and Defense, but apparently, someone thought FUCD was just too vulgar. Go figure. So FUC it was, the first line of defense for those who wore the fur all around the world. The avian and aquatic species had their own protective agencies that worked in close conjunction with FUC, and it wasn't uncommon for them to trade agents around, although nobody ever volunteered for the deep-sea missions, drowning on the job not exactly high on anyone's list.

"Serve, protect, and keep the humans in the dark." That was their motto, and as a FUC agent, she did whatever she needed to keep shifters safe, from guarding them to keeping humans ignorant to investigating crimes. A challenging job, yet she enjoyed the variety of her day-to-day tasks. And the dental benefits totally rocked.

Skipping over to the front desk, she leaned on its polished surface as she scanned the bulletins on the board. A wolf whistle made her whip up a middle finger before she turned with a smile. "Don't you have some pigs to bother?"

"I'd rather huff and puff all over you, darling," Frank replied with a laugh. Wolf shifter and lover of dirty innuendo, he flirted with anything classed as female.

"You couldn't keep up with me. Don't forget, the Energizer was my granddaddy."

A snorting laugh erupted from him. "You are a handful, Miranda. Hey, are you meeting up with us after work at Joe's Jungle for drinks?"

"Sorry, but this bunny is on a mission. Maybe next time." She tried to never drink on the job unless she needed to as part of her cover. Actually, even off the job, she didn't imbibe too much or often, given alcohol went straight to her head and made her hyper—and horny. She didn't want to wake up beside Gabe the snake again. Some things a girl was just better off not knowing.

"Did you manage to meet your target?"

Miranda finished signing in and spun to face the speaker. At well over six feet—yet considered small for her kind—Kloe, mission director and literal giraffe, towered over just about everyone, and had the longest, most graceful neck of anyone Miranda knew except maybe Jessie, their resident swan and tech geek.

"Phase one accomplished, boss. I've made contact with one grumpy, yet handsome, bear. He didn't look too impressed with me, though."

Kloe's lips curved into a smile. "Let me guess, you played the I'm-just-a-dumb-bunny for him, didn't you?"

Miranda batted her lashes. "Who, me?" She laughed. "Oh, you should have seen his face. I'm going to do the good neighbor thing tonight and bring over some home baked goods."

"Perfect idea. We all know how bears love their treats."

Oh, the bear wanted a taste of something sweet all right, but she'd recognized the look in his eye. *I think he wants a bite of a bunny instead of honey.* That would have to wait, though. She tried not to mix work with play—often. However, once she'd completed her mission, watch out, Chase Brownsmith. Not only did she plan to make him smile—maybe even chuckle— she had a hankering to see if grizzlies were as *big* as they said. "I'm assuming Victor took up the tail once my target left the building?"

"He did. Nothing to report as of yet. The crew is at his place right now planting the bugs—bedroom, kitchen, living room, and hall. His office was done last night. According to Jessie, you should have a link to your laptop and cell by this early afternoon, but we both know there's still nothing better than hands-on and eyes open wide."

"Oh don't you worry. I intend to stay stuck to that bear's ass better than a burr." Once Miranda got an assignment, in this case protecting an oblivious grizzly, she didn't stop until the job was done. "Any luck on finding out more about that list?"

Kloe shook her head. The list she spoke of, which

had arrived anonymously at their offices less than two weeks ago, contained the names of almost fifty shifters. All single males in tip-top shape. It would have seemed like a great source for eligible bachelors, except over a dozen of those men had gone missing in the last six months. Only one ended up recovered, dead, decomposing, and a cross between horrifying and nightmarish.

The tentative consensus was someone appeared to be kidnapping healthy males to experiment on. Why, who, or how remained unknown at this point. Heck, they still didn't know how they'd gotten the list of possible victims, but anonymous or not, FUC didn't sit idle on the clue.

In an effort to curb the disappearances, and catch the perpetrators, each of the names remaining on the list ended up assigned a pair of secret agents to watch over them. They didn't want to tip the perpetrator off that they were onto them, but at the same time, FUC couldn't stand by idle and waiting to see if anyone else got snatched. Miranda drew the job of onsite guard, while Victor, her partner, became the outdoor shadow. Between the pair of them, they were tasked with keeping the bear safe. Not an easy task given their sparse numbers, but that's where the surveillance would come in handy.

Debate on whether or not to notify the victims ended up with a wait-and-see approach. The fear was, if told, they might trigger some alpha male tempers, which would then force the perp to seek out new victims. Some might argue they used the males as bait. Miranda, though, preferred to think of it as secret volunteering because, surely, if the big, strong guys knew of the targets on their backs, they'd have agreed. Besides, if they did their job right, none of the targets would have to know.

While her subject worked in his office—out of sight and reach for the moment—Miranda took the opportunity to practice her protective and, if needed, deadly skills. When it came to guns, knives, hand-to-hand combat and more, she might appear cute and defenseless, but show her a bad guy and she'd pulverize his ass while smiling.

And, if all her training and weapons failed, watch out because she could always resort to her bunny side.

Chapter Two

Chase's tummy rumbled, and he looked at the time. Almost one o'clock and well past time for lunch. Lumbering out of his office, he noted his brother still hadn't come in, or so he assumed given the lack of lights in his brother's space.

"Katy, where's Mason?"

His receptionist looked up from her magazine, her desk neat as a pin without a single piece of paper left for processing or filing anywhere, and shrugged. "He called and left a message last night. Said he had to leave town for a few days. His schedule was pretty clear, so I assume it was for pleasure. He did sound kind of out of breath. Maybe he's found himself a hot female."

Brows drawn, Chase grunted at her answer. "Irresponsible cub. If you do hear from him, let him know that I'm still waiting on the Peterson documents."

"They're in your inbox."

Chase glared at her. "Stop working so hard. I just gave you a raise."

Flashing some pointed canines, Katy smirked. "And I am worth every penny and more. Now go eat. You're getting testy."

Grumbling about superefficient secretaries with no respect, Chase exited the office building and headed up the street for his favorite sushi place. Raw fish sounded real good right about now. Of course, nothing could beat the satisfaction of a fresh catch, but he couldn't deny that getting it served on a plate sure beat standing in a freezing cold river waiting to swipe one of the tricky bastards.

Ordering the usual smoked salmon, spicy tuna, a miso soup, and rice—in duplicate—he sat back and waited for culinary perfection. To distract his growling stomach, he whipped out his BlackBerry and pulled up the news headlines to read.

"Yoo hoo! Remember me? Your new neighbor."

The familiar voice made him groan. How could he forget? Despite himself, he couldn't help looking up. The bubbly bunny, still wearing her ridiculously short bottoms, waved at him with a brilliant smile. Chase fought an urge to flee as she headed his way, and he soundly cursed technology. *If I'd been hiding behind a real newspaper, she probably would have never seen me.*

"Are you meeting someone for lunch?" she asked, standing close enough for the scent of her to tickle his nose and reignite his arousal.

"No." Wrong answer. She took that as an invitation. A scowl in her direction didn't stop her from plopping her delectable ass on the seat across from him.

"What luck running into you here."

"I knew breaking that mirror would turn out bad," he mumbled.

Apparently, Oblivious was her middle name. "Do you work nearby? I just finished a round at the gym," she gushed, drawing Chase's gaze and making him notice the light sheen of perspiration on her skin. "I walked by this place and thought, sushi. I've always wanted to try sushi. So in I walk, and, bam, there's a familiar face."

"I thought rabbits were vegetarians."

A giggle rolled off her full lips. "Only the really skinny ones. I'm a meat and potatoes girl myself. And dessert. Mustn't forget a *creamy*, decadent dessert."

The way she said it made his cock harden and throb. He knew just what kind of cream he'd love to put in her mouth. *Bad bear.* He didn't know what it was about this female that made him randier than, well, a bunny, but he didn't like it one bit. "So are you taking your lunch to go?" He tried not to sound too hopeful.

"What, and leave my neighbor all by himself? How rude would that be?"

Not at all, he wanted to say, but the words remained caught in his throat as she bounded up from her seat and yanked on her shorts, tugging them from the vee of her crotch. It should have struck him as unclassy, far from ladylike, but all the could think of was, *Damn, wish I was the one wedged up there.*

"Darned wedgie," she griped with a chuckle. "I think my ass finally got too fat for these shorts."

"I think your ass is just fine." Chase almost looked around to see who'd spoken. Surely, he'd not just given the bunny a compliment. Judging by her pleased expression, he had. *Shit.*

"Why thank you… You know, I don't think you ever gave me your name."

Did he have to? "Chase."

"Mmm, Chase. What a fabulous name. I bet you get girls asking you all the time to chase them through the woods." She winked as she said this, and an instant mental video flashed of him bounding after the curvy, platinum female—naked of course—the round globes of her ass jiggling. He snapped his jaw shut before he drooled.

To distract himself, he absently asked, "What's your name?"

"Guess," she replied with an impish smile.

"Mindy. Bambi. Barbie. Jinx. Mercedes. Sasha." Chase held back a grin as he named off some exotic dancers he knew, not intimately, but through his work. They'd filed a class action lawsuit against the strip club they worked for, citing unsanitary work conditions and sexual harassment. It was what you got when a bar, catering to male wolves, didn't have enough bouncers in place. He'd tried to stay out of it, as that type of legal wrangling wasn't his usual fare, but the dancers clamored only he would do because, apparently, all the other lawyers kept trying to charge them in favors—the sexual kind. Chase settled for cold, hard cash.

She pouted at him. "I wish my name was so cool. My mom named me Miranda. How boring is that?"

A serious name for a flaky bunny. Go figure. "It's nice."

"Nice is another word for boring. Ooh, look, our food is here."

Our? Chase saw only his order, not that it stopped Miranda from sliding one of the bowls of soup her way.

It took great effort for him not to growl—and bat her hand away from his food. He didn't like to share. However, watching her purse her lips and suck her soup—with a truly dick-hardening suction—he let it slide. He could always grab some more honey buns on his way back to work.

"Mmm, yummy soup," she exclaimed, smacking her lips. "Now, I need to try some of this sushi stuff. Raw fish, huh? It won't make me sick, will it?" she asked, uncertainty clouding her features as she held up, between her chopsticks, a slice of salmon.

"They wouldn't sell it if you couldn't eat it. Dip it in the sauce and then pop it in your mouth." Chase led by example, the tangy taste making him rumble with satisfaction.

"Okay, neighbor. Here goes nothing." Dunking her piece of fish first, she hesitated a moment before she slid it in her mouth. She tried to grin as she chewed, and chewed, and chewed some more, but the look soon became forced. Chase snickered as he held out a napkin.

"Spit," he ordered.

She snatched the napkin from him and indelicately hocked into the tissue before scrubbing at her lips with a repeated, "Eeew."

"How could you not like it?" Like, seriously? Salmon was akin to ambrosia.

"It was cold and slimy, and icky."

He shook his head. "What did you expect? It's raw fish."

She stuck her tongue out at him in reply. Oh, the things he could do with that thing.

He drew his attention back to his platter. "Fine, don't have any then. It makes more for me." He dug in while she made gagging noises, which he easily ignored.

"I think you owe me dessert for that."

His brows raised in bewilderment as he tried to follow her logic. He couldn't. Swallowing, he tried to prevent himself from asking, but his curious bear nature demanded an answer. "How do I owe you dessert? You were the one who said you wanted to try it."

"You should have warned me I wouldn't like it."

He stopped eating and stared at her. *She's nuts.* "I just met you this morning. How the hell would I know what you like?"

She stuck her lower lip out and pouted. Personally, he could think of better things to do with those lips, but he kept them to himself.

"I guess you're right. I mean, why should you care, after all, if I'm new to the area and don't know where to find the yummiest desserts?"

Okay, rude and disgruntled bear didn't translate into a mean one. It occurred to Chase he could argue with her some more because it was actually pretty entertaining, or he could just give in to the inevitable and buy her dessert. After all, he needed something sweet to calm him down after this fiasco.

"Fine. But let me finish my lunch first."

"Perfect." She beamed, all smiles and sunshine again.

Apparently, her dislike of the fish didn't extend to other parts of his meal. Miranda inhaled one of his bowls of rice while he downed the platter of sushi with exaggerated groans of excitement. Her occasional frown and dirty looks made him chuckle inside. It seemed his dour demeanor was finally getting through to the bunny. He couldn't help himself. Cheerfulness just wasn't in his nature, a fact his mother lamented and his brother ridiculed.

Chase had always held a serious view of life. In his world, a bear should work hard, eat a lot, and sleep even more. Friendships took away from those three tasks and, in the case of food, expected sharing.

One day, still several years in the future, he'd settle down with a sow and pop out the customary cub or two. He already had a list of requirements for a mate—quiet, tidy, a good cook, and easy on the eyes. In other words, boring and not likely to disrupt his life. His brother, who'd heard his list, snorted he needed a housekeeper. He never repeated it after Chase knocked his front teeth out. Calm and controlled didn't mean he didn't have a wicked left hook. Back to his wish list, there was nothing wrong with wanting a docile partner who wouldn't interfere too much in his life.

Not like a certain bunny who would probably make each day a new adventure where he'd have to fight to keep his sanity. Where he'd be expected to share his food and bed while being subjected to inane chatter. Where the sex would be copious, sweaty, and frantic. *Why oh why can't I stop thinking of her like that?*

Done with their meal, Chase stood up, and Miranda joined him as they left. "Where are we going for dessert?" she asked, bouncing around in her too-short shorts. "Can we have ice cream?"

Chase almost said no until he thought of seeing her licking a cone. Logical or not, he couldn't miss that. His inquisitive bear side demanded to see it. He lumbered down the sidewalk, Miranda skipping at his side, chattering nonstop. "So how long have you lived in the area?"

"About five years."

"Really? I've actually lived here my whole life, but I was living on, like, the total other side of the city. Which used to be fine, but then my work changed location, and it occurred to me that I was wasting, like, two whole hours a day commuting, so I moved."

"You work?" Not that he really cared, but again, his bearish need to know made him ask.

"Of course I do, silly." She giggled. "And you'll never guess as what."

Pole dancer, waitress, daycare provider. "Supreme court judge?" he said dryly.

She stopped skipping and whirled to face him, halting his plodding steps. "Oh wow, do you think I could aspire that high?"

An unexpected heat suffused his cheeks as Chase realized she'd taken his words at face value instead of the sarcasm he'd meant. A real jerk would have pointed it out. "I think you can be anything you put your mind to." Diplomatic, and it seemed to satisfy her. *And is so unlike me. Since when do I care about hurting anyone's feelings?*

A slow grin spread across her face. She winked. "You're right. I can." She whirled around and resumed bouncing. It took Chase a moment to realize she'd never told him her occupation. *I don't care.* He bit his tongue before he could ask her and she really thought him interested in her.

What a relief when they reached the ice cream parlor, and she shut up for about five seconds. Chase held back several sighs as Miranda oohed and aahed over every flavor, unable to decide until he growled at her, "Hurry up and decide or I swear I'm going to find out if it's possible to drown a person in it."

Again, she stuck out that pink tongue of hers. "Oh please, like you'd waste that much quality ice cream when you could just throttle me." She said it with a smile that almost made his lips quirk in reply. He flexed his fingers at her, and she laughed instead of running away. Disgruntled, Chase didn't follow through because she finally made her selection.

Settling on praline butterscotch for him and bubblegum for her, they exited the store, nibbling on their treats. Actually, Chase almost choked on his when his eyes caught the agile swipe of Miranda's tongue swirling around the tip of hers before engulfing it. In and out of her mouth, she sucked. Chase could only stare in fascination while his cock engorged and begged to switch spots with her cone. *Sweet Ursa.*

It took the wet drip of his own ice cream melting and rolling down over his hand to snap him out of his trance. In a few bites, he'd disposed of his own dessert, and with a rushed, "Gotta go. I'm late for work," he escaped her, the soft sound of her chuckles trailing after him.

However, it was the image of her hollowed cheeks that haunted him the rest of the afternoon— and left him with a bad case of blue balls.

****

Miranda watched Chase flee and followed at a slower pace, knowing Victor waited ahead to pick up the trail, meaning Chase was in no current danger. *Unless a hard-on counts.* Her poor bear. He might not want to like her, but his body sure did. A feeling reciprocated, she realized, given her own soaked panties, tight nipples, and racing heart. *Uh oh, I think I'm starting to like the grumpy bear.*

Her decision to ambush Chase at lunch wasn't preplanned. She just couldn't resist seeing him, even though she hated fish—both the cooked and newly discovered uncooked variety. She placated herself with the false assurance that she was just getting to know her target. *Yeah, I now know he's deliciously hot, owns the sweetest blush, and a body that I want to ride all night long.*

Returning to the office, she diverted her thoughts from Chase by immersing herself in their current mystery. In the case of large operations, a special room was set up with all the pertinent facts so that individual agents working different aspects could browse and, if lucky, draw correlations between pieces of evidence. The current war room's four walls were plastered with pictures of all their victims, missing and not. Below those images were notes on what they knew about the missing shifters and their last known locations. Needing a place to start, she first studied the cases of the ones they couldn't locate.

What they all shared in common was size. They were big alpha males who wouldn't have gone down without a fight. While the FUC agents couldn't exactly pinpoint their disappearances, all the evidence pointed to the victims vanishing without anyone noticing. No signs of struggle. No traces of anything, blood, hair, or otherwise. Some type of incapacitating drug appeared to be the general consensus, but how was it being administered?

It was while she perused the names that she noticed a disturbing fact. Mason Brownsmith, Chase's brother, had a big question mark penned in beside his location card. Apparently, no one could find the bear, and Miranda's stomach sank. *Oh no, please don't tell me the bad guys already got him.*

She wondered if there was a way she could unobtrusively ask Chase if he knew his brother's whereabouts. How to find out without divulging what she knew? She'd figure something out.

Mason wasn't the only target missing. Two others on the wall appeared unaccounted for, although, in one case, it appeared the subject might have gone on vacation to Mexico.

Miranda left off her contemplation as Kloe called a meeting of the agents in the office to apprise them another body had turned up, just as misshapen as the previous one. Miranda held on to the contents of her stomach, barely. The images of the new corpse flashed on the screen for everyone to see. Not everyone could handle it, and a few operatives ran from the room, the faint sound of their retching making everyone left behind squirm uncomfortably.

"We have to stop whoever is doing this," Kloe said in the silence that followed. "Remember, everyone, serve, protect, and keep the humans in the dark, but, most important of all, stay safe."

Meeting ended and close to five o'clock, Miranda decided not to press her luck and "accidentally" run into Chase while he walked home. Not after the way she drove him nuts at lunch. However, she did use thoughts of him to distract her from the disturbing news at the meeting. As it turned out, it wasn't hard to focus her mind on him.

What an intriguing bear/man. On the exterior, he appeared like his animal, big and gruff, but every so often, she caught a glimpse of the inner teddy, the soft one who displayed a wry humor—and scorching , if restrained, passion.

Not ignorant of her own charms, and using them

to her advantage, she couldn't miss the smoldering interest in his gaze or the toe-curling heat radiating off his body. *I'll wager, if I'd have groped him, I would have found one extremely hard dick.* She wondered if riding a grizzly would compare to riding a bull—the mechanical sort that was.

Chase, however, wasn't on the menu for sex. Not until he became just a neighbor instead of her target. *I'd better work quick on solving this case then if I intend to not blur the line between business and pleasure.*

The first thing she did when she got home, after taking a shower where her removable spray head was used in ways never intended by the manufacturer—or was it?—she jumped onto her laptop and signed into her encrypted account with FUC. She easily pulled up the cameras in Chase's apartment, only succumbing to a slight twinge of guilt as she watched him blithely go about making his dinner—a roasted honey glazed ham with mashed potatoes and honey-glazed carrots.

Her tummy rumbled, and her mouth watered as he sat down, alone with a pile of mail, to eat a meal more fit for two. After all, a little bunny like her wouldn't consume that much. Surely he could share? Seeing his intense look of enjoyment as he swallowed, though, she refrained from going over to invite herself for dinner. Barely. Anything that could give a man such a sinful expression deserved a place in her belly.

Watching him with more interest than a man simply eating deserved, she noticed his lips masticating and move independently of each other, a really weird bear trait she'd read about but never noticed before, even though she'd shared lunch with him. *I wonder if he'd wear that same rapturous expression using those dexterous lips of his on my pussy?* The simple thought of it soaked her panties. Not one to resist the urge to masturbate, she quickly shrugged off her shorts and panties. She splayed herself on the couch, her legs propped and spread for easy access. Staring at Chase's image, she felt only a moment's shame at using him as the focus of her sexual fantasy. But the naughtiness of touching herself without him knowing soon blew that twinge away.

It proved easy to imagine his mouth sliding down her body, those flexible lips of his nibbling her flesh. In response to her visual imagery, her hand slid down her frame. She raked her fingers through her curls, picturing him nuzzling her pubes, inhaling her scent. One finger grazed over her already sensitized nub, a fleeting caress that made her channel tighten. In she dipped a finger, wetting it before taking it back to swirl against her nub.

Still seated at the table, Chase reached for the carrot bowl and knocked over his water. She watched with heavy eyes as he jumped up, the faint sound of his curses ringing through the speakers. He stripped off his shirt, and Miranda's tongue almost lolled out like a dog's at the sight. Bulky muscles rippled all over his thick torso. Add in the fact he was wide-shouldered with well-defined pecs and abs she could worship, the sight of his flesh teased her for a moment before he sat back down to finish his meal.

And Miranda finished herself. While the fingers of one hand plunged into the moistness of her sex, the other frantically rubbed at her clit, the quick pace heightening her tension until, with a small exclamation, her climax hit. The shuddering ripple made her body seize and tighten around her inserted fingers. She closed her eyes and sighed in pleasure as she rode the quivers.

A knock on the door jolted her out of her pleasant reverie, and she scrambled to find her shorts.

"Who is it?" she called as she hopped into her bottoms—pantyless and sticky-thighed.

"Me."

Miranda almost fell over trying to put her leg into the hole of her bottoms. *Chase? What's he doing here? Don't tell me I screamed his name aloud when I came?*

Peering at the monitor, she noticed his empty apartment, but on the fifth screen, showing the hall, she saw him standing with a letter in one hand.

Yanking up her shorts, she quickly buttoned and looked for something to wipe her still damp hands on. Spotting nothing useful, she ended up settling for the ass of her shorts. *Mental note to self, these bottoms need to go in the wash.*

A knock sounded again, and she could almost hear the impatience in it. She slapped the laptop lid down and took a few deep breaths before opening the door with a chirpy, "Hey, neighbor."

Intent brown eyes met hers, along with Chase's customary scowl, but she didn't let her own smile falter, not when she could feel her spent orgasm soaking the crotch of her shorts.

"The mailman gave me this by accident."

"Oh, thanks for bringing it over." He held out the plain white envelope, and Miranda, suddenly much too aware of her own sticky fingers, reached out to grasp it. It would have been too much to hope that he wouldn't catch the lingering scent of pussy on her, but he, of course, did, and his brows beetled together.

Her cheeks heated under his perusal then turned to lava when he inhaled deep. "Am I interrupting?"

Miranda didn't see the merit in lying and actually impishly looked forward to flipping the tables with the truth. She tossed the mail behind her and held up her hands, waggling the fingers. "Nope, just me and my ten fingers." His attention caught, she put one digit in her mouth, sucking it slowly while his eyes widened. "Finger-licking good. Want a taste?" She offered up a sticky finger and almost laughed as his face grew tight. Hunger flashed in his eyes then ruddy embarrassment followed by sultry heat. A man of many faces.

"I prefer my honey from the source, but thanks." And with his shocking statement, Chase turned around and went back to his place, leaving her standing with her jaw hanging wide and her crotch revving up again.

Hot damn. That kind of statement takes balls. And she'd bet his real ones were just as big as the rest of him. She shut the door and leaned against it, her heart pounding. It was as she took her second shower that it occurred to her she had the best excuse in the world to go knocking on his door again.

I did, after all, promise him a treat this morning as an apology for waking him up this weekend.

As soon as she hopped out of the shower and dressed, she got to work measuring and mixing. Irrational, foolhardy, but that didn't stop her. Bears weren't the only curious creature, and this bunny wanted to know what it would take for one grumpy bear to kiss her or, at the very least, crack a smile.

Chapter Three

Hand delivering mail shouldn't be enough to drive a bear insane. Or so Chase thought when he handed her the envelope he'd accidentally received and got a whiff of the sweetest scent ever.

Miranda should count herself lucky she didn't lose her finger. A bear could take only so much temptation. After he'd blurted his unexpected comment of eating from the source—*Where the hell did that come from?*—Chase just about ran back to his apartment, his cock jerking in his pants. If his dick could have spoken, Chase swore it would have said, *"Hey, the pie is the other way, dumbass."*

The worst part? His cock had a point. When Miranda offered him her digit, covered in her very own brand of honey, he almost took it and her entire hand in his mouth to lick it clean. The smell alone transcended heavenly into must-have. Even now, with the door shut, and him leaning against it, he panted and just about drooled, knowing the sweetest dessert waited for him just across the hall. One lick, who could it hurt?

She's trying to drive me insane. He'd known her for less than a day, and already she'd wreaked havoc on his carefully ordered life. Worse, she kept waking his curiosity, a bearish trait he'd worked long and hard to stifle. Curiosity killed the cat and, in the case of a bear, got him into trouble. Just look at that damned Yogi. Okay, maybe the Hanna-Barbera cartoon was fiction, but he knew for a fact it was a bear who wrote the script based on his own adventures in a national park. In Chase's case, it wasn't picnic baskets or honey tempting him into trouble, but bunny pie. Sweet, tasty, hot bunny pie.

Hunger swamped him. He strode back to his dining table and sat, trying to rediscover his appetite, but the only thing that demanded feeding was his damned libido. Chase grumbled and stomped as he plastic wrapped his leftover meal, not something that happened often at his place. The mundane task should have settled him, but oh no. All he could think of was Miranda across the hall. Miranda naked with her legs spread wide so he could eat her sweet pussy. Miranda bent over so he could plow her moist sex. Miranda screaming his name as she clawed his back in the throes of orgasm, her wet honey soaking his cock.

Five hundred pushups and three hundred and seven sit-ups later, he still found himself horny as hell. He welcomed the distraction from his carnal thoughts, which arrived in the form of the knock at his door. He whipped the door open without checking first—perhaps to avoid disappointment if it wasn't a certain platinum-haired neighbor.

Excitement made his heart speed up as he beheld her, wet hair slicked back, looking freshly showered—how unfortunate. His regret that she'd bathed only lasted a millisecond as a heavenly scent wafted up to him, and he peered down to see a pie. A real, beautiful, lightly-brown-crusted pecan and honey, whipped-cream-topped pie. *Don't let her see you drool.* The reminder helped him snap his mouth shut, but the saliva still pooled.

"Hey, neighbor. I bet you thought I forgot," she said, thrusting the dessert up at him.

"What?" He couldn't take his eyes from the steaming dessert with the heavenly aroma that made his stomach growl.

"I told you I'd make it up to you, and I always keep a promise. I baked you a honey pecan pie."

Chase almost said, "Marry me." Seriously, the words were on the tip of his tongue. She'd made his very favorite dessert, and it smelled even better than the one his mother made at Christmas, and on his birthday, and, well, anytime Chase went home. "Thank you," was all he managed to utter as she transferred the still warm dish to his hands.

Mine, all mine. My precious. Impatience to taste it made him silly, almost drunk on the fumes of the baked honey. He turned around and was about to kick the door shut with his foot when she spoke. "Aren't you going to invite me in so I can have a piece with you? I wouldn't mind sharing a bite."

Share? But he wanted it all for himself. Chase looked down at the pie and then peered back at her. She grinned. A devilish idea—unlike his usual churlish ones—formed in his mind. Setting the pie down, he scooped a finger into it, the heat of the filling almost too hot to handle. Scalding or not, he popped it into his mouth anyway, almost dropping to his knees in pleasure as the sweet honey flavor hit his tongue. *Oh sweet Ursa, it tastes better than it looks.*

He couldn't wait to take his next bite. However, even amidst the tummy-tingling pleasure, he didn't forget his primary purpose. He moved quickly back to Miranda, only vaguely noticing her widening green eyes. Before she could say a word—a rarity in her case—he placed his hands on her waist and lifted her up. *What do you know, I was right. She's just the perfect size for hoisting,* was his last coherent thought before he slanted his mouth across hers. Electricity of the carnal kind arced between them.

Is it me or are there fireworks going off? His fantasy of how she'd feel paled in comparison to the reality. She fit against him perfectly, her lush curves an ideal complement to his hardness. Her mouth pressed softly against his, her initial surprise yielding to sensual reciprocation. Chase pushed her up against the wall of his entrance, his lips moving in opposing directions against hers, wanting to memorize every inch of her.

Her lips opened wide in a startled gasp, and he used that opportunity to slide his tongue into the warm recess of her mouth. He thrust his groin against her, and her legs parted to wrap around his waist, drawing him right up against the heat of her. A groan escaped him, swallowed by her eager mouth. Her arms twined around his neck as he deepened the kiss, the electrifying embrace firing all his senses. It was more drugging than any honeycomb. More arousing than any other kiss he'd experienced. More delicious than any pie.

Pie?

Thoughts of the pie, the scent of which still tickled his nose, snapped him back to awareness. *What the hell am I doing?* It was with shock he realized he held Miranda pressed against the wall, her legs locked around his waist, her core rubbing against his turgid cock. It would be such a simple matter to tear the cloth between them and take her. Sink himself into her glorious pussy. Worse, he knew it would feel so good.

But it wasn't what he'd planned. His loss of control shook him. Unwinding her from his body, he set her back on the floor in the hall, his breathing just as ragged as hers.

"There's your taste. See you later," he managed to mumble, ignoring the wakening shock on her face. It hurt him to shut the door in her face, but what proved harder was not throwing her over his shoulder and dragging her into his cave.

Remember, she's a bunny. A long-eared woodland creature and not an appropriate partner. His cock didn't agree. Chase growled.

Closeted in his apartment, his balls so freaking blue they were liable to fall off, he sat down to eat his pie, which paled in comparison to the taste of Miranda's mouth and her passion.

Dammit. Since when do I want to trade my favorite pie for a piece of ass? Swollen cock or not, he still managed to eat half the confection before frustration made him stop.

Chase took a cold shower, and when that didn't shrivel his swollen dick, he jerked off several times until finally, his prick almost raw, he fell into bed. However, even in his sleep, he dreamt of only one thing—Miranda. And oh the things she did to him, and he to her.

He awoke with a shout the next morning to the shrill scream of his alarm, his sheet damp and his cock limp. A wet dream? He couldn't remember the last time he'd enjoyed one of those, and it should have embarrassed him, but he found himself, instead, somewhat relieved, if sticky.

As he showered off the traces, he unfortunately couldn't stop his mind from straying, not to what he'd have for breakfast, lunch, or dinner. Well, unless he counted Miranda's pie as a meal. And dammit all, if his dick didn't try to lift again. *This won't do at all.*

After a breakfast consisting of a box of Honey Nut Cheerios, several bananas, the rest of the yummy pie, and a carton of orange juice, he dressed for work and came to a decision that made him feel a whole lot calmer.

It occurred to him that his unnatural attraction to Miranda had a simple solution. Sex. Not with her, of course. How awkward would that be given their neighbor status? Despite the fact none of his usual casual lady friends appealed, he'd bite the bullet and go out with one tonight. At one point in the evening, he'd do the dirty deed. Maybe more than once given how his apparently dry status had driven him to this chaotic state in the first place.

And then, once I've taken care of my libido, I'll be able to ignore Miranda instead of kissing her senseless. Decided, a tranquil peace settled over him

Serenity only extended so far, though. Ready for work, he squinted through his peephole and checked the corridor to ensure nothing dangerous lurked.

Not seeing any sign of a perilous bunny, he grabbed his briefcase and keys then opened the door. In his haste to secure his door and escape, he fumbled at the lock, distracted by her lingering scent, which grew stronger the more he inhaled. After several tries, with a firm click, he managed that simple feat and turned. Then yelled.

"Hey, Chase," said Miranda, beaming up at him, a twinkle in her green eyes. "Are you going to work too? Why don't we walk together?"

"Um. Uh." Cohesive sentence structure and simple English escaped him as the fiery memory of the kiss they'd shared—and the even naughtier dream he'd enjoyed—made his body flare to life. She took his lack of response as acquiescence. Looping her arm in his, she just about dragged him to the stairwell.

"I usually take the elevator," he finally managed to say through gritted teeth, trying to fight his body's immediate response to her nearness, namely a raging erection and insane urge to hoist her so he could taste her luscious lips again.

"Why would we do that? We'd miss a chance for some exercise. Come on, you lazy bear. Or are you afraid you can't keep up?" She winked at him, the challenge clear in her smirk and bright eyes.

A bear did have his pride. "Fine. We'll take the stairs." Then, before he could think twice about it, or even question what prompted him to do it, he grabbed Miranda and threw her over his shoulder. Arm secured over her thighs—unfortunately clad in jeans—he entered the stairwell and began to jog down to the sound of her giggles.

"Is there a point to this?" she exclaimed between fits.

"Weren't you the one claiming I needed exercise?"

"Yes. I did, didn't I? Well then, mush, my big ol' teddy bear. Mush." She punctuated her gleeful shouting with pinches on his ass. Hard pinches that made him growl, but, surprisingly, not in anger. Funny how Miranda could get away with doing things that would have made him tear a strip off anybody else.

He jogged down faster, her body bouncing up and down, making her breathy squeals *oomph* out of her. The sound really piqued his imagination as he could so easily picture it coming out of her in so many different other scenarios, naked ones, of course. Dirty thoughts he just couldn't seem to stop.

When she slapped his ass and screamed, "Faster," he slapped hers right back. It seemed like the thing to do.

The wrong thing for him as it turned out because the faint scent that he'd come to associate as uniquely hers multiplied by like a thousand. Her bottom, already so close to his face, oozed arousal, and it took more restraint than he cared for to resist turning his head sideways to take a bite of her—or, even better, throw her up against the wall and plow her.

He dumped her on her feet in an abrupt motion that made her grunt and sway. He meant to flee at that point, claim he was late for a meeting and run as fast as he could. Instead, he leaned in and stole a kiss, a hard, bruising one as if to punish her for making him feel this way.

The damned cottontail wench, though, didn't retreat, or complain. She threw herself right into the embrace. In moments, they were both panting and grinding against each other.

"This is wrong," he grunted as he palpated her ass, his tongue swirling around the shell of her ear.

"Definitely," she murmured. "We really should stop." And with those words, she pushed away from him, turned, and walked away.

Chase stared after her, dumbstruck—and harder than a freaking rock. Chasing after her wasn't an option—the whole pride thing. A growl escaped him. *Tease.* Never mind he'd started the kiss. It was up to him to decide when to end it.

Just one more reason to get his loving elsewhere. A female bear wouldn't have walked away. She would have taken care of his needs.

I don't need Miranda for satisfaction. As a matter of fact, maybe instead of going out for once, I'll make dinner at my place for the lucky sow.

And he knew just who to invite. Kerry, the screamer.

Chapter Four

Miranda jogged to work sightlessly, utterly muddled from the scorching kiss Chase had planted on her. Walking away took every ounce of willpower she owned—plus some. However, after the way he'd ditched her last night after getting her all hot and bothered, he deserved it. Payback was a bitch, though. Just ask her complaining pussy.

She didn't worry about Chase being left behind without her to protect him, not when she'd seen Victor lurking across the street waiting to pick up his tail. Frazzled, she didn't even respond when Frank whistled at her as she reached the FUC administration level. Instead of bantering, she fled to her cubby space and flopped into her chair, staring at her blank computer screen.

I have got to get myself under control or take myself off the case. It only belatedly occurred to her just how oblivious the kiss had rendered her. The kidnapper could have walked in on them and zapped them with a Taser for all she'd have noticed. *I probably would have mistaken the electrical jolt for the sizzling connection I have with the big ol' bear.*

No doubt about it, she liked Chase. She could almost claim obsession because she wanted to know the taste of him and how he'd feel *in* her, *on* her, *over* her. Her turmoil was such that she'd neglected to pump him for info on his brother. Speaking of whom, maybe the agency collected some information on him overnight. She hopped up from her chair and made her way to the war room, welcoming any chance at distraction. Once inside, surprise made her do a three-sixty, her eyes frantically scanning the space, only to realize Mason's information was gone.

"Looking for something?" Kloe's voice came from behind, and Miranda turned with a frown.

"What happened to the info on Chase's brother?"

"We no longer need to concentrate our efforts on him."

How ominous sounding. "He's—he's not dead, is he?" she asked, sadness creeping over her at the thought of poor Chase losing his only sibling.

"No. Why would he—you know what? Never mind. Turns out, he's not a shifter we need to focus on. On the other hand, you've got a target you do need to worry about. Anything to report on that front?" Kloe's gaze zoned in on her, and Miranda fought an urge to fidget.

Anything to report? Hmm, other than the fact Chase was an awesome kisser and ditched her for pie? "No. Nothing yet. But it's been only five days since the last abduction. The other ones were about two to four weeks apart."

"Our profilers seem to think whoever is doing this will start accelerating the process. They're predicting a snatch before the end of the week."

"Not on my bear they won't," she replied with more vehemence than she intended.

Kloe's face crinkled with concern. "Everything all right, Miranda? You seem a little out of sorts."

A sigh slipped from her. "Ever meet a man who makes your legs wobble like Jell-O and makes your heart patter so hard it feels like it's coming out of your chest?"

"Yes."

Miranda shot her a questioning look. "What did you do?"

"Married him, of course."

Miranda reeled back from the answer. "But what if he disliked you? Or at least acted like he did one minute and kissed you the next?"

A smile spread across Kloe's face. "You wouldn't happen to be talking about one sexy bear, would you? Jessie mentioned something about a hot liplock when she peeked in to make sure the monitors were all up and running last night."

Blushing fiercely, Miranda hopped from one foot to the other. "Yeah, well. Did she also mention how he got me all hot and bothered then dumped me in the hall to eat some pie?"

"Was it your honey pecan? If yes, then, I'd have to say, tough call."

Miranda shot her a glare. "Great. Make me feel better, why don't you? I got him back this morning, though."

"I'm afraid to ask how."

"When he kissed me again and then said he shouldn't, I said he was right and walked away."

Laughter burst forth as Kloe erupted. "Oh, that would explain why he was snarling at everything in his way this morning and came out with twice the amount of honey buns from the bakery. Victor wondered if something had happened."

Somehow, knowing she'd thrown Chase off kilter made her feel better. A whole lot better. She went about her morning tasks, keeping an eye on her monitors showing Chase's outer office. They hadn't bothered with his inner one, given the only access to it was from the reception area.

When she saw him leave for lunch, she bounced out of the office, intent on intersecting him. However, instead of going to eat, he went to the grocery store. Puzzled, Miranda followed him in, but held back, ducking behind aisles every time it looked as if he would turn and see her. He picked up and paid for a multitude of items, including flowers.

Interesting. She dodged his footsteps as he dropped his purchases off at his apartment. But he didn't stay there. Off he went again on another errand. Shadowing him, she watched him stop at the liquor store. She placed herself across the street, browsing a street vendor's wares while unobtrusively keeping an eye for Chase to emerge.

"Trying to steal my job?" Victor's low voice made her jump.

She squeaked. "Would you stop sneaking up on me? You scared at least ten years off me."

"But sneaking is what I do best." Victor grinned at her, his wide smile displaying way too many teeth, a crocodile trait that took some getting used to. While not furry like some of the other agents, Victor was a welcome addition to the FUC family.

"So, any idea what he's up to?" she asked as she watched Chase saunter back out of the liquor store, bag in hand.

"Hmm, off work early, flowers, food, and booze? He's getting ready for a hot date."

Miranda's lips curved into a smile. "I think you're right. I wonder who the lucky lady is," she said coyly. "I gotta go."

"Whatever. Have fun."

Miranda almost bounced like Tigger all the way home. Chase was going to surprise her with a romantic dinner. It made walking away from his scorching kiss this morning worth it. But, if she was going to be ready, she needed to get hopping. First things first, time to get out the razor. She had some serious shaving to do.

A few hours later, dressed casually in easy to rip off clothes, her face artfully done, she watched in disbelief on her laptop monitor as he opened the door to a coiffed and statuesque female.

That jerk. Irrational jealousy made her angrier than she ever recalled. *Why should I care if he invites women over? He doesn't belong to me, kiss or not.* Her inner pep talk didn't stem her annoyance. Watching the monitor, she got more and more annoyed.

I am such a dumb bunny. And here I thought he was going to try and seduce me. Apparently, the kiss they'd shared left more of an impression on her than him. Fixated on the unfolding—heartbreaking—scene of seduction, she ground her teeth when Chase patted his date's hand. Not exactly an intimate gesture, but still, he'd touched her! She slammed the laptop lid down when she saw the sow simper up at him, her lips puckered for a kiss. Before Miranda could think twice, she'd stormed out of her place and banged on his door.

When Chase opened it, a smug look crossed his way too good-looking features.

"Jerk." She socked him with a clenched fist in the gut. Then stomped on his foot for good measure.

"Ow! What was that for?" he gasped.

"I'm a woman. I don't need a reason," she spat before pivoting and marching back into her place. She slammed the door for good measure. Then, she sat and glared at it. She ignored the temptation to peek at the monitor and see what happened over at Chase's place.

With her luck, she'd catch the two-timing jerk laughing about the crazy bunny across the hall or, worse, doing the horizontal tango.

I need a drink. Unfortunately, all she had was some leftover peppermint Schnapps from Christmas. Two shots later and she was on her ass on the floor, singing eighties love songs, and not very well.

****

Chase stared at Miranda's retreating back and flinched when she slammed the door hard enough to rattle the frame.

What in Ursa's name was that about?

There was no mistaking Miranda's pissed—seemingly jealous—state, but how had she known about his date? Kerry arrived less than half an hour ago, and while they'd talked, Chase never even reached the point where he made her scream in orgasm. Actually, he wondered if he would have even have gone through with the plan. Seeing Kerry again, he hadn't exactly found himself overcome with lust. Heck, he ended up faking interest and fought not to cringe when she brushed against him. He'd tried to touch her, on the hand to start, but a sense of wrongness made him snatch it away. He'd almost run with relief to the door when the furious pounding started.

Seeing Miranda, her eyes flashing and her hair a silken sheen that smelled of sunshine, his elusive hard-on returned with a vengeance, and in that moment, he'd wanted her so freaking bad. Then she'd hurt him, or tried to. It didn't actually work, and the fact she'd even tried annoyed him. But not as much as Kerry.

"Who was that rude woman? And why was she hitting you?"

Did she deserve an answer? Chase looked at Kerry's haughty features and wondered how he'd ever found her attractive. "Leave." He handed Kerry her coat.

"What? But what about dinner, and you know…" She winked and licked her lips.

A shudder went through him. Nope, so not interested. "Yeah, well, that's off."

"Is it because of that—" She inhaled. "Bunny?" she finished with distaste.

"Don't talk about Miranda that way," he growled.

"Fine. Go and cavort with the little lettuce eater. See if I care." With a sniff, Kerry took herself off.

Relieved he wouldn't have to fake a hard-on for the sow, Chase went into the kitchen and stared at the dinner he'd prepped all afternoon. It wouldn't do to let it go to waste now, would it? After all, it wasn't his fault his date went awry and he couldn't get an erection for a perfectly fine sow.

However, sitting down to eat, he couldn't find his appetite. The food sat like tasteless lumps in his mouth. Opening the wine, he poured himself a large glass, downed it, and poured another. Soon, he skipped the glass and just drank straight from the bottle, ruminating on what was wrong with this picture. He actually had a list starting with his blue balls, followed by his perfectly fine dinner going to waste, then his failed date, which led back to his blue balls.

It's all that bunny's fault. Ever since he'd met her, things had been going wrong—and hard.

Before he could talk himself out of it, he marched out into the hall and banged on her door. She didn't answer, but he could hear sound, similar to that of an animal being tortured. Frowning, he banged again.

"Miranda. Open up. I know you're in there."

"Scrrrrew. You," she answered with a mighty slur, and then broke out into an off key version of Madonna's "Respect Yourself.*"*

Talk about cruelty to animals. "I'm going to take this door off if you don't let me in," he warned.

"Why don't you go back to your—your date," she yelled. "You two-timing bear."

A twinge of guilt almost made it into his somewhat inebriated brain, but frustration quickly doused it. "That's it," he grumbled. "I'm counting to three, and if you don't open the door, I'm breaking it down so I can wring your little bunny neck in person. One." He ignored the rational part of his mind that said he was acting like a rabid bear.

"You can't do that," she hollered.

"Two." He listened to her moving and could swear he smelled her just behind the wood.

"I haven't done nothing. Go away and harass your date," she cried.

"Three. Ready or not, I'm coming in." He moved back a pace and dodged forward, but he never got an impact as the fuzzy wench flung open the door with a smirk and stood aside as he barreled through. Halting his momentum, with skidding feet on her wood floor, he whirled to face her, his chest heaving as he panted.

Miranda glared right back, her arms crossed over her chest. "I let you in. Now leave."

"You ruined my date."

"Good."

His eyes narrowed. "You aren't going to apologize?"

"For what? Saving her from a guy who kisses a girl one day then makes dinner for another the next?"

"It's your fault that happened," he growled.

"Exactly what part?" she sassed.

"If you didn't smell and taste so damned good, driving me freaking crazy, I wouldn't have had to make her dinner and try to get laid."

A puzzled look creased her face. "Okay, now you lost me. Want to explain that in English?"

"I don't want to want you."

"So don't," she replied tartly, but not before he caught the glimpse of hurt in her eyes.

"It's not that easy apparently. Kerry was supposed to fix that problem."

Miranda's eyes widened. "You were going to boink her just so you could forget me? I don't know whether I should be flattered I have that kind of effect or clobber you over the head for being a jerk."

"How about not looking so damned cute to start with?" Her mouth opened and closed as she stared at him incredulously. Chase snapped his shut as it finally filtered through his thick head what he'd said. A groan escaped him, and then a second when her face went from pissed to delighted, a smile lighting her face.

"Ha, I knew it. You do want me."

"No, I don't," he corrected. "I just don't seem to currently have a choice."

"So what's the big deal? I'm willing to get naked if you are." She winked at him, and an instant erection tented Chase's pants.

"No. No. No. This isn't going to work. I'm a bear. You're a bunny. Two completely different species."

"And? Last I heard, so long as we're in human shape, all our equipment is compatible." She cocked her head at him. "Don't tell me you've never boinked someone outside of your animal group before."

"Not since college. It's best not to become attached to someone unsuitable," he stated firmly.

"And you think I'm not suitable?" she queried, that hurt expression back in her eyes.

"Not suitable for me. Perfect for anyone else." Although the thought of her with anyone else made him want to burst out of his human skin and go on a murderous rampage.

"I see. So, you think you're too good for me. Nice to know. But here's a clue, Baloo. While I'm sure we'd have a great time in the sack, you are too much a stick in the mud for me to ever become permanently attached to. So, you wouldn't have to worry about me clinging. I never thought we'd enjoy more than a few rolls in the hay before we both went our separate ways. Although, now I think I'm going to even forget the sweaty sex."

She spoke so seriously that it threw Chase for a loop. What happened to his bubbly bunny? *I broke her.* Not only that, he'd managed to talk her out of curing the problem in his pants. A problem she admitted she would have willingly taken care of, no strings attached.

There was only one thing to do.
Fix my bunny and change her mind.

Chapter Five

Chase advanced on her, his eyes narrowed with intent. Miranda squeaked, not really in fear, but sudden excitement of the chase, by Chase. She giggled, the alcohol not completely cleared from her system even though her rapid metabolism worked at it.

After her confusing conversation with Chase, one thing became clear, even to her fuzzy brain—*he wants me, but wishes he didn't.* On the one hand, she found it flattering she drove him crazy with desire—especially since she reciprocated that desire. However, hearing that her bunny genes just weren't good enough for anything other than casual sex pissed her off. Never mind the fact that she wasn't looking for anything permanent. Now that he'd effectively tossed down the gauntlet, she, number one, wanted to make him lose control and take her—what fun. And number two, she perversely wanted to change his mind about the whole interspecies thing.

Grumpy, outspoken, fish-loving lug that he was, she wanted him. *I'm just afraid one night won't be enough.* She liked Chase—a lot—which meant, no matter how much fun his seduction would feel—*oh the naked, sweaty pounding of it*—if she gave in, especially after his statement that her genes weren't good enough for him, how would she ever get him to respect her? It surprised her how much his acceptance meant to her. It surprised her even more that she hadn't yet tossed him out on his ear for his insult, though.

Retrospect aside, there was still one horny bear in her apartment. She hopped away from his clutches, springing over her furniture agilely while he lumbered after. He didn't say a word, his heavy breathing and her panting the only sounds.

"I think you should leave," she huffed as she nimbly ducked under his arm and scurried to the other side of her living room.

A grunt was his answer, compounded with a naughty glint in his eyes that went well with the partial curve of his mouth. *Ooh, he's not making this easy, the cute devil.*

"Seriously, Chase. Since you feel so strongly about the whole interspecies thing, then I think it best you go now before you do something you'll obviously regret." *But so definitely enjoy.*

"I'll regret it more if my balls fall off," he grumbled.

His words caught her by surprise, and she missed a bounce. She hit the couch, and before she could scramble up, he lay atop her, his heavy body pinning her. His large hands clasped hers and raised them over her head, trapping her beneath him, placing her at his mercy.

How decadently delicious. She placated herself with the knowledge she'd tried to foil his seduction. What a shame. She'd failed. She would now take her punishment as she deserved—right between the legs.

Chase didn't immediately kiss her, though. His brown eyes gazed into hers. "What is it about you that drives me crazy?" he asked. His tone and expression were pensive—although his cock, pressing against the juncture of her thighs, certainly knew what it wanted.

"It's my cute button nose and freckles. They act like an irresistible lure, kind of like a siren's song," she replied, slightly breathless and not because he crushed her. She liked the weight of him on her. Stranger, she even liked that he fought his attraction to her. Most males just tried to seduce her with no care for tomorrow.

"I've known good-looking women," he answered, still studying her features. "None ever invaded my every thought and dream."

Her mouth rounded into an O of surprise. "You dream of me? For real?"

As if suddenly realizing he'd spoken aloud, Chase clamped his lips tight, and a shuttered look came over his face. They stared at each other for several moments more, but even in the silence, a connection forged between them that, while unseen, she could almost feel—and it linked straight to her heart. Whatever his thoughts on the matter, she understood in that moment that what drew them together transcended lust. *Does he sense it too?*

Perhaps he did because Chase kissed her. Not the teasing, sugary kiss of the night before, nor the scorching punishment of the morning. No, this embrace imparted pure sensuality. He caressed her lips with a reverence that made her tingle all the way to her toes. Touched her as if she was the most delicate and precious thing he'd even encountered. He explored her lips slowly, his mouth teasing and nipping, driving her completely mindless with erotic sensation. *I could stay like this forever.*

The tip of his tongue slid forth to trace the seam of her mouth then delved into its recess as she parted her lips. The soft sound of their mingled breaths filled the air interspersed with her moans of pleasure as he took his time kissing her.

Pleasure uncoiled in every nerve of her body, especially between her thighs. Pinned, she could do nothing, not even arch against him, but he knew what she wanted. Read her body with his own. He ground himself against her, the hardness of his cock, even with the layers of fabric between them, pressing on her core, driving her wild.

She wanted to feel him inside of her, pounding at her flesh, his body meshed to hers. She wanted…the damned phone to stop ringing.

With a groan, Chase pulled his head away, his eyes smoldering with lust. "Don't you have voicemail?"

No, but she suddenly made a mental note to get it right away. Interrupting that kiss bordered on sacrilegious. "I don't have voicemail. I just moved in and was too cheap to get it. Hold on. Let me get rid of whoever it is."

Chase let her up with obvious reluctance, and she scurried to answer her ringing phone.

"Hello," she answered, smiling over at Chase, who lay on the couch with his hands linked under his head. Damn, did he look good there, his eyes half shut with languor, the prominent bulge of his cock calling to her.

"Miranda, oh good, I caught you. Sorry to call you at home, but your cell wasn't answering," Kloe said, reminding Miranda she needed to charge it. "Listen, did you get the package Jessie sent over?"

Miranda's brow crinkled at Kloe's question. "Package? What package?"

"On your kitchen table. Jessie brought it in earlier."

Miranda held a finger up to Chase and mouthed, *Give me a minute.* Wandering into her kitchen, she scrounged through the mail and newspaper she'd tossed on her table when she'd come in. She located the small box and opened it. It contained a small ring box inside. Flipping it open, she stared at the tiny round disk no bigger than the end of her pinkie nestled in its depths.

"Did you find it?" Kloe asked.

"Yeah." A knot formed in her stomach. Knowing Chase probably listened, Miranda turned on the kitchen tap, the splashing water masking whatever she and Kloe now said to each other.

Oblivious to the havoc going on in Miranda's mind, Kloe made a pleased noise. "Excellent. Jessie came up with a GPS tracker for our subjects. It's a stick on patch that will allow us to find them if they accidentally get snatched."

"Won't our subjects notice we've chipped them?" Miranda queried, the sick feeling in her tummy increasing. "Or are we now telling them what's going on?" *Please.* Honesty was surely better at this point than tagging the male in her living room about to make love to her. *If I care for him, then I can't keep lying about who I am and the danger he's in.*

"Nope, mum's still the word. You just need to get close enough to your subjects to stick it somewhere they won't notice. It should last through several showers and whatnot before it needs replacing. Will you have any problems getting it onto your target?"

Holding in a sigh, Miranda answered. "I've got it. Anything else?" *Like, say, stabbing myself with a dagger?* It would probably hurt less than the continued subterfuge.

"No, that was it. See you in the morning."

"Yup, see ya." Miranda hung up and looked at the small disk, which acted as a cold reminder of why she'd even met Chase. *How could I have lost sight of my objective?* Chase wasn't a potential boyfriend or lover, but a possible victim in need of protection. In her lust—and irrational jealousy—she'd lost track of that important fact. Kloe, though, had inadvertently reminded her. Conversation over, she no longer required privacy, and Miranda turned off the water, fighting an urge to cry.

If she told the truth, she could jeopardize the whole operation and put both agents and targets at risk. However, if she continued to lie... *Then I might discover firsthand whether the advice to never get on a grizzly's bad side is accurate or not.*

The situation sucked big time, but she at least went into it eyes open, if stupid. Poor Chase, though, he didn't have a clue. *And I can't make it easier by telling him.* She had a job to do, whether she liked it or not. Once the situation with the kidnapper was resolved, then maybe she could tell Chase about her part. See if he would forgive her for doing her job. *If all else fails, I could always resort to those damned shorts again, along with some more honey pecan pie.*

Decision made, even if she didn't particularly want to celebrate it, she snagged the chip onto the end of her finger, its translucence making it almost invisible. She peeled off the wax backing and took a deep breath as she prepared to chip her bear.

Striding back into the main room, she pasted a smile on her face. "Sorry about that. It was my mother. She always has the best timing."

"Why do I get the impression the mood is blown?" he asked wryly as he stood up.

"Yeah, well, hearing about her menopausal symptoms will do that to a girl," she said with a shrill laugh. "Anyway, sorry I ruined your evening."

"You're lying to me. What's really wrong?" His piercing gaze saw right through her, and guilt made her drop her gaze.

"Nothing." *Except for the GPS tracker on the end of my finger and the enormous lie of who I am.*

"I see." His low tone just increased her guilt. He turned to leave, and she bit her lip, looking down at her finger.

"Chase." She said his name softly, but he pivoted immediately. She made her way across the room in a rapid walk and flung her arms around his neck. She tilted her face up and gave him a smacking kiss to distract him from the pinkie pressing into the skin between his shoulder blades. "I truly am sorry. Good night." She let go and stepped back, closing the door into his brooding countenance before leaning on it. She slid to the floor and blinked away the tears.

Why did she feel like the biggest fraud alive? *Probably because I just micro chipped the guy who, only moments ago, was about to boink my brains out. He's right. I am so wrong for him, just not for the reason he thinks.*

****

Back in his apartment, Chase sat down and admitted to bafflement. One minute Miranda was moaning and ready for him, and the next, she turned into an aloof stranger who couldn't get him out of her place fast enough.

He didn't understand her one bit. *Why do I even care? I'm not looking for a relationship. Heck, I wasn't even planning on having sex with her, although I'm kind of bummed it didn't happen.* Would plowing her sweet pie have cured his insane desire for her? Somehow, he doubted it.

He lusted after Miranda to the point that he couldn't think clearly. The blood in his brain appeared to have taken up permanent residence in his cock. And his cock wanted to take up residence in her pie.

Actually, so did his tongue and fingers.

His reaction to her baffled him. Desire like he'd never known kept swamping him, whether she was present or not. Worse, despite his general dislike of all things perky, he found himself enjoying her presence and her quirky outbursts. He looked forward to her smartass comments and her infectious bubbly laughter. Stranger, the things he enjoyed about her didn't have anything to do with the naked tango. *Oh for Ursa's sake, I like a damned bunny.* A temporary insanity? How could he find out?

There was only one solution left—other than moving to Siberia. He'd have to do the bunny. And in do, he meant fuck her six ways from Sunday, in every position possible until his balls shriveled up and fell off. Surely, once he slaked his thirst for her, he'd finally be able to return to his regular—staid and boring—life.

He ignored a niggling doubt that once he had a taste of Miranda, he'd never be able to enjoy bland again.

The following morning, he exited his apartment for work, expecting to see Miranda bounce out at him. He kind of counted on it, actually. When she didn't, he tried to tell himself he didn't care. *I am such a liar.*

All the way to work, he kept stopping and turning, certain he saw a glimpse of platinum locks or heard her giggle, but each time, it ended up some stranger, and his dejection grew, giving credence to his theory that perhaps his mind had gone off the deep end.

He forwent his usual honey bun morning pick-me-upper and buried himself in his work, the tediousness of all the paper dulling his mind and irrational hurt at what he considered a snub.

Apparently, Miranda could do what he didn't have the heart to—move on.

Lunch arrived, and his tummy rumbled loud enough that he couldn't ignore it. Despite his dejection, he needed to eat. Heading to his favorite taco joint, he ordered the works, plus some. Food always acted as a balm when he was troubled. Fate must have taken pity on him because he'd no sooner gotten his order when Miranda walked in wearing a skirt that, surprisingly enough, didn't bear any drool marks—yet—and made him want to cover her up. The idea that any males on the street could admire her rounded calves and creamy thighs roused a possessive growl out of him. He could just imagine what she would expose if she happened to bend over.

It was more than a bear could handle. He acted while she bounced up and down in place on her sneakered feet, placing an order at the counter.

Sneaking up on her—a bear hunting his prey—he

softly rumbled, "Yummy, rabbit for lunch." Before she could react, he spun her and kissed her. Her rigid shock melted quickly into soft compliance, her lips yielding under his with a matching passion and hunger.

A cleared throat made Chase raise his head and bark, "What?" He glared at the server, who swallowed hard.

"The lady's order is ready."

Chase snatched the bag and dragged her back to his table. "Sit."

A bemused expression on her face, she plopped herself down across from him. "Yes, sir. Now what?"

"Eat with me." Wiped from his mind were the reasons to avoid her. Seeing her just made him realize how much he wanted her, needed her around him.

She cocked her head, a ghost of a smile teasing her lips. "I thought you preferred to eat alone."

"Don't throw my words back at me. I'm a man. It's my prerogative to be ornery."

White teeth gleamed as she laughed. "I like you...*ornery*. But I need to get back to work."

"What exactly is it that you do?" he asked.

"I'm a super-secret spy on a mission to save the shifter world," she replied with a straight face.

Tease. Chase scowled. "Fine. Don't tell me."

"You wouldn't believe me if I did."

"Would you believe I'm a lawyer?"

She laughed. "Hmm, I would have never guessed, what with the suits you wear and the I'm-a-serious-bear outlook you seem to have on life."

"Nothing wrong with being a proper professional. I guess you'd prefer my brother, Mason, then. He's more like you, never taking anything serious."

"You have a brother? Are you close?" Her eyes dropped and stared at the table where she traced circles with her fingers.

"We work in the same office, but don't really hang out. Heck, he's been gone for a few days now doing Ursa knows what and didn't even bother leaving a note. I guess that goes to show how close we are."

"That's a shame. I've got two sisters and three brothers, although I'm the only bunny like my dad. I see them every holiday and birthday. My family loves to party, and our motto is the more, the merrier. And even though they live in another state, I talk to them all the time."

"That sounds busy." Chase almost shuddered at the thought of that many family functions. He visited his parents a few times a year, but other than his brother sometimes joining him, it didn't devolve into big parties.

"It's awesome. Maybe I'll take you to meet them sometime."

Chase tried to hide his look of horror, but, apparently, didn't quite succeed.

She shook her head as she chuckled. "Or not. I keep forgetting. You like being a grumpy old bear."

Not so grumpy around you, though. He kept those words to himself, but couldn't stop himself from saying, "Have dinner with me tonight."

"I can't."

"Why not?"

"It would be a bad idea." Eyes tinged with sadness rose to meet his. "You were right last night. This thing between us won't work. We're too different."

"Since when are you the type to give up?" *Since when do I resort to begging?*

"Bye, Chase." She stood up and grabbed her bag of food. She turned to walk away, but pivoted back. She leaned down and embraced him, a sweet kiss that stole his breath and didn't hide the tears shimmering in her eyes. Then she was gone.

He tried to immerse himself in his food, the spicy tang of the taco sauce redirecting his focus for a while. That only lasted until he once again hit the street, her words and kiss—of goodbye?—plagued him.

I think I just got dumped. How can that be when we were never technically dating?

He wished he had someone to talk this over with, but with his parents on an arctic cruise, mingling with the polars, and his brother AWOL, he struggled alone. Not usually an issue, and how he preferred it, but for once in his life, solitude wasn't a soothing balm. He already missed the unexpected chaos of Miranda. The color she brought into his life...the passion.

In a bear's world, more specially Chase's, when emotions created havoc in his heart and mind, there was only one cure—sugar. Entering the bakery, he ordered some honey buns. A new employee, a greasy-haired teen, reached under the counter and yanked out a bag.

"Here you go."

Chase frowned. "Are they fresh? Usually they pull them from the display."

A nervous smile flitted across the kid's face. "They were expecting you and told me to bag them up ahead of time."

That made sense. Having missed his morning pickup, they'd probably reserved some for him as a just in case. Chase paid and exited the store, the sweet smell making him lick his lips in anticipation. The brief swipe of his mouth brought to him the faint, lingering flavor of Miranda. His lips tingled at the remembrance of her kiss—and his cock throbbed, a permanent state since he'd met her.

I should thank her for halting things last night and making things even clearer today. What was I thinking? A little bit of lust and I was ready to go against my principles. But what if my morals are wrong? Is it really that important for me to keep my bloodlines pure? And an even better question is, what makes me think she's the one?

After all, he'd bedded plenty of sows and never thought about going to the next step. Then again, he'd never felt one iota of the things he'd experienced since he'd met Miranda. He could almost predict now that one taste of her would never satisfy him. And then where would he be? Doing the one thing he'd sworn he wouldn't, diluting his lineage.

But at least I'd be happy—if possibly certifiably insane living with a crazy bunny. Somehow, the idea didn't frighten him as much as it should have.

Of course, he also had an even bigger stumbling block than his own prejudices—Miranda, who no longer seemed keen on getting involved. Then again, just look in any shifter dictionary and you'd find a picture of a bear under the words stubborn and persevering—and Chase just happened to own both those qualities in spades.

Entering his office, he noticed Katy preparing to leave. "Where are you going?"

"I have a dental appointment. Let me guess, you forgot? I've put sticky notes on your desk for the items you need to deal with today."

Seeing his brother's still-dark office, he frowned. "Any word from Mason?"

Katy paused at the edge of her desk, and a line of concern creased her forehead. "Nope. Did you want to file a missing bear report?"

Did he? What if Mason was simply having sex, lots and lots of it? Would he thank his brother for interrupting? "Not yet, but if he doesn't call in the next twenty-fours hours, I think we might have to."

Katy left, and Chase entered his office. He dropped his bulk into his chair, which creaked alarmingly. Damned things kept breaking on him. Annoyed, Chase yanked a bun out of his bag and chewed. He ate three before a sense of calm settled over him. A yawn erupted from him, and he rubbed his eyes.

It seemed his lack of sleep the last few days had caught up with him. He pulled another pastry out and ate it slowly, the fatigue clutching at him tightly until he could fight it no longer. His big head thumped forward, hitting his desktop, but his body numb, he didn't feel any pain.

It occurred to him that something about his rapid and unwilling descent into slumber appeared unnatural, a fact reinforced by the thumps and stealthy movement in his outer office.

Consciousness took too much effort, and sleep, with jaws tighter than any predator, grabbed him and took him down into oblivion.

Chapter Six

A warning bell went off on her cell phone, and Miranda, buried once again in the war room photos looking for a clue, jumped. She whipped her phone out and pulled up the message alert.

Camera six, location Chase B. office, offline.

She'd no sooner pulled up that monitor to confirm when another bell went off, and another.

Camera three, location Chase B. living room, offline.

Camera one, location Chase B. hall, offline.

After the third message, she didn't bother looking anymore and started jogging to the elevators as she dialed Victor's number. It went straight to voicemail, and Miranda's heart stopped beating for a second before adrenaline kicked in.

"Code Red," she hollered as she reached the main FUC vestibule, but she wasn't the only one yelling codes. Agents were pouring out of their offices screaming for backup as phones all over the place went nuts.

"Cameras are all down," yelled someone. "Tracking teams are not answering."

Seeing Kloe standing amidst the chaos with a scowl on her face, Miranda snagged her attention. "What the heck is going on?"

"Someone's cracked our system and infiltrated part of the network. They've taken most of our monitoring cameras down. Jessie's working on routing the hacker out and getting our firewall back up."

"So we're under attack?"

"A tech attack only as far as we know, but until we get our eyes and ears back, you need to get to your subject ASAP and make sure he's safe."

"I can't get a hold of Victor either."

"Probably more of the hacker's work because there isn't anyone alive who could catch that croc off guard."

It only takes once, Miranda thought as she watched everyone scurrying. What a great diversion if someone intended to use the chaos to snatch some males. Miranda took off again, hopping in the elevator with other grim-faced agents.

"I can't get a hold of my tracker," she said as the cab started to move.

"Me either," replied Helen. "And of course the cameras are down. I've got a bad feeling about this."

"You and me both," Miranda muttered. Panic made her heart race as she imagined Chase in danger. *Don't worry, my grumpy ol' bear. I'm coming to protect you.*

As soon as she and the other agents hit the lobby, they raced out the door, ignoring the questioning looks of the humans. Once on the street, they split up, Miranda sprinting to Chase's office building. She had the doors in sight when Victor melted from the shadows of an alley.

"What's the hurry?" he asked.

"The cameras are down, and I couldn't get you on the phone."

Victor yanked his cell out and frowned at it.

"What are you talking about? It doesn't show me missing any calls."

"Hackers got into central and messed everything up. Since our phones run on a FUC network, I guess they got caught up in it. Anyway, I was just going to check on Chase in person."

"He just went in about an hour ago with a bag of those pastries he seems to like so much. His secretary left not long after, but I haven't seen him or anything suspicious in the meantime."

The nagging sensation that something wasn't right demanded she see him for herself. "I'm still going up."

"I'm right behind you then."

The lobby to Chase's office building didn't contain anything suspicious, so they went to the elevator and headed straight up. Exiting into the carpeted and silent corridor, Miranda didn't need Victor's finger over his lips to know to keep quiet. The doors on this level were all shut, the various plaques announcing their occupants the only color in the grey space. They moved on silent feet to the end of the hall, but even before they reached Chase's door, Miranda's nose twitched.

"I smell shifters. At least three of them and, judging by the fresh scent, not that long ago."

Victor, whose crocodile's senses didn't extend to smell, took her word for it. "Could be some clients," he replied, doubt in his voice.

They both knew better, though. The pit in Miranda's stomach, also known as her instinct, screamed something was awry. Victor went through the door first while Miranda covered him from the corridor, her pistol drawn and pointed. She'd felt naked these last few days without it on her person, but given her undercover status, she feared Chase seeing it and asking questions. Besides, she didn't need bullets to cause some damage. She had herself.

Victor gave the all clear, and she entered. She saw no sign of struggle, but judging by Victor's grim face, they were too late.

"He's gone?" She needed confirmation before she completely flipped out.

Victor held out a bag from the bakery. "I took a lick, and while I don't recognize what drug they used, these are definitely laced if my numb tongue is any indicator."

"They put him to sleep with a tranquilizing agent and then snatched him. But how the hell did they get him out of here without anyone seeing?"

Victor dropped to the floor and pinched something between his fingers. He held it up for her to see.

She blew out an annoyed breath. "A piece of lint? So what?"

"Carpet fiber," Victor explained. "I bet you they wrapped him up in a piece of carpet and carried him out through the back service door."

"I thought you could see both entrances from your spot," she barked, placing her hands on her hips.

"I could, and I even saw the guys who took him and the roll your bear was probably in." He held up a hand before she could yell at him. "These guys are good, though. The carpet guys have been working this place for two weeks now, coming in and out with carpet, a legitimate building reno by the owners. I know because I checked."

"And yet you didn't notice they were shifters?"

she said, her sarcasm biting.

"They weren't until today," he snapped back. "Now instead of getting your panties in a twist because lover boy is gone, why don't you act like an agent and help me find him?"

The verbal slap made her recoil with shame. She'd taken her frustration out on Victor because of the guilt swamping her. *Maybe if I'd paid better attention to my job instead of how to get in Chase's pants, this wouldn't have happened.*

"Sorry. You're right. This is my fault."

"I didn't—"

She cut him off before he tried to absolve her. "No, it is. And now because I screwed up, I need to work twice as hard to get him back."

"But how? You and I both know the carpet place will be a dead end. The kidnappers probably ditched the van within a few blocks."

"Ah, but I have an ace up my sleeve that I'm hoping they don't know about." Miranda tucked her gun away and pulled out her cell to call Jessie.

It rang six times before a harried voice answered. "I'm a little freaking busy right now," Jessie honked, her agitated bird side making itself known. On loan from the avian division, everyone relied on Jessie when it came anything to do with electronics.

"Yeah, well, when you get unbusy, I need you to track my target. This whole thing with the cameras and phones was a smokescreen so they could snatch my bear."

"What?" Miranda held on as she heard Jessie mumbling about no-good hacks who deserved to have keyboards shoved where the sun didn't shine. Jessie came back on the line. "Lucky for you, I've got the new tracking system on a whole other server. I didn't want to bring it online with the other stuff until I knew it was ready."

"Are you saying I chipped my bear with untested hardware?"

"Not completely. I used it on Frank first, and believe me, the places he went... Eew, let's just say the device performed well. I see no reason why it wouldn't work on your bear."

Miranda ground her teeth, resisting an urge to reach through the phone and throttle the swan's long neck. "So does that mean you can find him?"

"Probably, unless he ends up in a lead-lined cell. You'll need to give me a few minutes, though. It's kind of a mess over here. Meet me in my computer room in like ten minutes and I should be able to help you."

Jessie hung up, and Miranda looked over at Victor, who grinned, his excitement evident. "I guess we're going on a rescue mission."

"Freak. I know you. You're dying to try some new gun out, aren't you?"

Victor's smile widened. "Who, me? Maybe. Just wait until you see what this baby can do."

Miranda shook her head. Boys and their toys. At least with Victor at her side, she stood a chance against whatever the kidnappers might have in store for her.

Well, short of an army anyway, but even FUC wasn't oblivious enough to miss something like that.

****

Fog clouded his mind. A nauseating disorientation that made him blink his eyes and shake his head—or try to.

Oh, what a bad idea.

His stomach churned, and he held on to its contents by sheer force of will. Breathing deep, in through his nose, out through his mouth, Chase pushed back the debilitating dizziness and managed to open his eyes. What he saw didn't make sense, so he closed them, counted to five, and then opened them again.

Nope, he still didn't recognize the concrete walls, the steel door, and, even more disturbing, the other male hanging from manacles on the wall. A tug on both his hands made it clear he wore the same kind of jewelry.

Great, kidnapped by some bondage freak. Chase didn't allow fear to control him, not when he still found himself more curious about the situation. Besides, he was a freaking grizzly. There wasn't any chain set in concrete that could hold him if he got pissed enough. However, before he went on a rampage, he wouldn't mind knowing what he was up against.

"Psst." Chase's version of a whisper came out like a muted rumble of thunder.

The other guy didn't move a hair.

"Oh for Ursa's sake. Wake up."

Nothing—well, from the other male in the cell with him anyway. Outside the door, though, he heard the sounds of locks being pulled. The portal swung open, and two camouflage-wearing—which seemed redundant outside of the jungle—soldiers entered with rifles pointed. Behind them followed a third man dressed in jeans and a dirty T-shirt, but it wasn't his attire that caught his attention, rather the scent. Hyena. The most irritating of the shifters, and the most mentally unstable of the bunch, except for squirrels, who were at least harmless.

Chase didn't say a word as the carrion eater moved to stand in front of him. He let his narrowed eyes speak for him.

"Ah, the grumpy one awakes. I told them you'd need more of the drug than the others because of your compacted human size."

"What do you want?" Chase didn't have the slightest clue, although it embarrassed him to know his sweet tooth had landed him in this mess. *That's it, no more bakery treats for me.*

"I don't want a thing from you. My boss, however, does. He wants your body."

"Not interested. I'm not into perverted sex games." Chase couldn't prevent the distaste in his voice.

The hyena laughed, a shrill, high-pitched sound that didn't reassure Chase in the least. But he didn't let it show on his face. He needed every extra moment he could get as the drugs cleared out of his system, restoring his strength and clarity.

"Your dick is quite safe. Your genes, on the other hand, that's quite another story. We originally planned on nabbing your brother, but…well, that didn't go as planned."

"What have you done to Mason?" Chase growled, lunging forward. The chains, though, held him back from his smirking captor.

"Nothing unfortunately. But if I were you, I'd worry more about yourself. By midnight tonight, you'll be on a plane to your destiny, and if your fate is anything like the others', let's just say you should enjoy what time you have left."

"You little bastard. You aren't going to get away with this."

"Yeah, funny how I hear that a lot, and yet, look at me. Not a single scratch, and what do you know? I'm also not chained to the wall, full of drugs." With those words, the hyena pulled something out from his back pocket. A large syringe filled with a cloudy yellow liquid. "Say goodnight."

Chase tried to swing his body to the side to avoid the needle, but manacled in place, his body still too sluggish from the previous drugs to obey him, he couldn't stop it. The syringe entered his skin, and the hyena pushed down on the plunger.

Chase had only time to mutter a slurred, "Gonna fucking kill you…" before slumber took him away again.

Chapter Seven

Miranda hated waiting. Hated waiting for the bus, standing in line for her turn. Heck, she hated the two minutes it took for popcorn to pop. She liked to move, hop, and skip, not stand still in one spot. However, what she preferred didn't matter in this moment because she lurked outside the warehouse that Jessie's computer claimed held Chase. Given the choice between rushing in like an idiot, guns blazing, and risking his life, or hanging tight until Victor returned with a prelim report, she chose tarrying. Anything to increase their odds of getting Chase, and any other targets, out alive.

With the hacker routed, systems back up and running, and the dust settled, they discovered that out of three attempts in their sector to abduct, only two had succeeded. The shame of her target being one of them made Miranda seethe. Especially once she discovered the failed attempt had a lot to do with the fact that the subject knew—and had known since he started sleeping with his agent—of their operation and stayed on guard for treachery.

Kicking herself for not doing the same, though, wouldn't accomplish anything. She could allow only one goal to fill her mind—get Chase back. It wouldn't be easy.

Shorthanded, because they didn't dare pull agents off the remaining subjects in case of another round of abductions, Miranda was only one of eight FUC agents about to infiltrate the warehouse the tracking device led them to. They'd evaded the sweeping cameras as they closed in, each simply armed with a gun and knife, except for Victor. Knowing him, he probably carried an arsenal on his person.

Bouncing on the balls of her feet, body primed for action, she waited as Victor and another operative slipped inside the deceptively quiet building, their objective to locate and disable any alarms and sentries. While they took care of the first part of their infiltration, the rest of them, including Miranda, monitored the various exits.

A heavy stench of ammonia, a liquid used to clean the glass, made and stored in the warehouse—a valid business front from what Jessie could tell— made their duty even more onerous, and probably explained why no one had reported any shifter activity in this zone.

A shadow slid from the side of the building, and Miranda brought her gun up, her finger lightly resting on the trigger. She recognized the shape and walk of her partner even before Victor's whispered, "It's me."

"What did you find?" Miranda kept her real question—*Did you find Chase?*—to herself.

"Something is going on in there. They've got way more security cameras than a place like this should need. I shut those down and turned off the motion alarms."

"What about opposition?"

"I came across four guards in total, three of them human and dressed in fatigues, carrying standard military-issue rifles."

"You think the government is involved?" she asked, appalled.

"No. These are hired guns."

"How many more do you think are in there?"

Victor shrugged. "Couldn't tell. The main floor is set up like a business, but it looks like there's a network of tunnels and rooms under the building that didn't show up on Jessie's schemata of the place. Stranger, the cameras only monitored the upper level and surrounding area. So there could be no one down there, or there could be like a hundred mercenaries waiting for us."

"What does your gut say?"

"Definitely at least a dozen, I'd say, maybe more. But it's weird. Other than the one rat manning the security cameras, the guards were human. And Bo, who came with me, says the basement smelled mostly human too."

"So what do we do?" Did she go in with the agents on hand, blind and possibly outnumbered, or did she abort the mission and wait for backup to arrive in the next few days to perform a full-on raid?

"It's up to you. But if your bear is in there, this is probably our best chance. If they move him, we might never locate him again. Hell, he could already be gone. Jessie lost his signal not long after he got to this location. It could be he's buried too deep for her to read him, or they've removed his chip."

Miranda gnawed her lip with indecision. Kloe had left the operation entirely in Miranda's hands, trusting her to use her head instead of her testosterone. *However, I didn't count on my heart screaming at me to go in guns blazing.*

"Listen, I was talking with these guys on the way

over. Joel's ready to go in and find his subject, along with Frank. Bo is definitely game, and the others will follow if we tell them to."

"What do you think?"

"I think we have the element of surprise, which works in our favor."

"Fine. We go in. Make sure everyone knows. Oh, and try to keep a couple of the bad guys alive. Kloe will want to question them."

"Aw, ruin a croc's fun, why don't you." The teasing words made her smile for a brief moment before the severity of the situation made her grimace.

An unknown amount of opposition, a labyrinth of passages, and a trigger-happy reptile. What fun.

Victor jogged back over to the door he'd used to get in the first time and slipped in. A moment later, he let loose the signal, a warble that he thought sounded like a frog, but sounded more like her clogged sink. Miranda left her hiding spot and entered the building, the other agents falling in behind her. Once inside, she followed Victor, who waved with an arm toward a metal door, which opened onto stairs. She ignored the two bodies lying prone beside it, human sentries who'd not proven good enough for the job. Or at least not as good as Victor.

Down the steps they went in their bare feet, their shoes left with the vehicles before they began the mission to ensure silence—and rapid shifting.

Entering into a dank room with three branching corridors, Miranda looked to Victor, who shrugged.

"I can smell my subject to the left of me," Joel stated, his head veering in that direction.

"And there are hyenas to the right," Bo added.

"And mine's in the middle," said Miranda, anxiety making her want to rush to find him.

"This is starting to make me think of a song," Victor mumbled.

Miranda knew the tune he referred to from a bloody guy flick titled *Reservoir Dogs*. She preferred to stick to warmer titles like *Gnomeo and Juliet*. And she just loved how her mind wandered, trying not to think about what she might find. "Okay, there's eight of us, who knows how many of them. Joel, Frank, and Mary, you three go left and find your target. Bo, Kyle, and Stu, you check out the hyena situation to the right, discreetly please. You know those dirty creatures like to run in packs. Victor and I will retrieve my subject."

Nods of assent met her decision, and butterflies danced in her tummy.

"Oh, and be careful, would you? I don't want to have to fill out the paperwork if any of you decide to get killed."

Morbid humor achieved, they set off. Victor took point as the others fanned out in their respective directions. Miranda trailed Victor, the lack of ammonia down below allowing Chase's scent to filter through, interspersed with a few hyena traces, some rat, and lots of human.

The hallway curved left and right in a sinuous pattern with doors set every so often in its walls. The cinder block corridor lit by string bulbs seemed too quiet. Too easy. Miranda didn't like it at all, and neither did Victor.

"Something's not right," he whispered. "Why have only four guards above and nothing below?"

"I don't know. Maybe they knew we were coming

and left."

Victor shook his head. "No. They're here, but they're waiting for something. Any idea how much farther to your bear?"

"Close."

On they went a few more yards before Miranda stopped. Taking a deep inhalation through her nose, one that filtered the myriad odors, Miranda backtracked and pointed to a bolted metal door. "In here."

Victor made quick work of the locks, his skills many and varied. No one knew exactly who had trained him. Supposedly, he'd shown up at the agency one day and offered his services. Five years later, the croc still remained an enigma, but a fantastic field agent. And friend.

With a click, the portal swung open and Miranda peered inside, only barely holding on to a gasp. *Oh, my poor bear.* She approached Chase, who hung from the wall in chains. His head lay slumped forward, going well with his limp body. The rise and fall of his chest let her know he lived. A quick glance showed two more sets of manacles cemented into the wall, but while she scented another shifter other than Chase, the room was empty.

Victor darted a glance to her from where he stood in the doorway, watching the hall. "Can you try and wake him up while I go and see what the hell is going on? There's no way we can carry his ass without some help."

"Go. I've got this."

Victor swung the door shut partway and left.

Alone with Chase, Miranda ran her hands over his body, checking for any visible signs of injuries. Or so she told herself. The thick body remained unresponsive, but anger burned inside her that someone would have done this to such a prime male specimen. And that's what he was. A live specimen for some sicko who used shifters to run experiments.

"Not if I have anything to say about it," she mumbled.

She examined his chains, now wishing she'd asked Victor to stay long enough to unlock them. Then again, she thought with a moue of distaste, the wall he hung on was probably cleaner than the floor, which seemed to have a thick layer of dust and detritus.

"Chase," she whispered, gripping his cheeks to lift his head. That took more effort than expected. The man owned a heavy melon. "Oh honey bear," she crooned. "Time to wake up." She brushed her lips against his, hoping to see him stir.

Nothing, not even a twitch.

Sighing, she let go of his head and prepared to resort to more effective tactics. She gripped his sac and said a silent apology before squeezing—hard.

****

The sudden agony dragged him up from the pit of molasses his conscience had sunk into. He focused on the bright pain and fought back the layers of fatigue trying to pull him back down.

A worried voice buzzed in his ear. "So sorry, my grumpy ol' bear. I don't want to hurt you, but you need to wake up, and I'm all out of smelling salts."

Chase opened a bleary eye as the familiar voice caught his attention. "Mir-r-ran-d-da?" he slurred.

"Yes, Chase, it's me."

Soft hands palmed his face and lifted his heavy

head. Concerned green eyes stared into his, and enough sense came back to Chase to realize Miranda needed to go before she got caught too. "Ish dangerous," he mumbled with a thick tongue that wouldn't cooperate. "Leaf. Liv now." His garbled speech frustrated him, but not as much as she did when she didn't immediately comply.

"Oh, my poor honey bear. What did they do to you?"

Chase blinked and shook his head free, trying to shake the effects of the drug. "Tha poishoned meh honey buns."

"What did you call me? Honey buns?" She craned to peer at her ass, for once decently clad in waist-to-ankle cargo pants. A shame, less clothes would have probably gotten his heart racing faster. "Hmm, I guess I can live with that as a nickname. Although, I'd have thought you'd have gone with honey pie."

Her deliberate obtuseness irritated him, which, in turn, got his blood sluggishly moving. "Miranda," he growled. "This isn't funny."

"I know, but can I just say you do look awfully sexy in chains. I mean, just think of the things I could do to you," she said with a lick of her lips.

Well, that definitely got his blood circulating, just not to the right head. A little more of his reasoning power returned, and the incongruity of her having located him struck. "How did you find me?" he asked, his brows beetling together. He refused to even contemplate she might have taken part in his abduction. Although her very presence seemed damning.

"I told you I was a secret spy," she sassed with a wink.

I'm going to throttle her. Then plow her then maybe throttle her as I plow her. "This isn't a game, Miranda!" She ignored his shout to move across the room and stick her head out the door.

In the distance, the muted pop of gunfire made adrenaline surge through his body. He flexed his arm muscles as his strength returned and the effects of the drug wore off, but not enough for him to help her—yet. He strained at the chains holding him, grunting as he pulled.

She returned to stand in front of him, shaking her head. "Don't strain yourself, honey bear. We'll get those chains off you in a few minutes." Then she patted him on the cheek, as if placating him.

Since asking nice hadn't worked, he snarled. "Stupid bunny. You're going to get yourself killed. You need to leave. It's not safe."

"Yeah, so you keep saying, but what kind of neighbor would I be if I left? Sorry, my grumpy bear, but I am not leaving until I save your ornery carcass," she chirped. She ignored his frustrated growls to eye his manacles with interest. She ran a finger along the chain to the wall.

"This isn't some Peter Cottontail adventure or story," he hissed. "The guys who grabbed me are real badasses. I care about you, dammit, and I don't want to see you hurt."

Miranda stopped her inspection of his restraints and turned with an incredulous look on her face. "Wait a second, I thought you didn't like me. Well, me as a person, 'cause we both know you want my body."

"I don't. I shouldn't." At her crestfallen face, he sighed. "Okay, insane as it is, I do like you, and not just your body, but your irritating mind as well. Just don't tell anyone. They'd probably institutionalize me. Now, please, do me a favor. Go get some help before they come back."

A sly smile crossed her face. "I like you too, my big ol' bear, and guess what? I am the cavalry." She flexed her arms and struck a pose. "You're looking at a FUC agent in the flesh. And I am going to rescue that hot ass of yours."

A FUC agent? Was Miranda delusional? He almost said it aloud, but swallowed it as she yanked out a gun from a pocket in her pants.

"Who was insane enough to give you a gun? Put that thing down before you hurt yourself."

She blew him a kiss. "Don't worry, I don't miss. Often, that is." She took aim at his arm and cold fear swept through him.

"Miranda, I don't think that's—"

Bang! She shot the chain and split it only inches from the iron bracelet around his wrist, freeing one of his arms. Unfortunately, before she had time to shoot off the second manacle, the sound of thumping feet reached them.

"Get behind me," Chase ordered, a need to protect her surging through him. Even with only one arm free, he could cause some damage and use his body to shield her.

Miranda snorted. "And miss all the fun? Don't worry, honey bear. I'll protect your sweet cheeks, and then we'll go home for some honey." She leaned up on tiptoe and brushed her lips quickly across his before she turned and dropped into a shooting stance.

Arms braced in front of her, the pistol held steady, she was ready when the first guard burst through the door. Fifteen feet away and she nailed him between the eyes.

Lucky shot.

She also nailed the next three in the same spot, and Chase's jaw dropped in astonishment. *My bunny is a sharp-shooting killer!* Well, not his bunny, but still, you thought you knew a cute woodland creature's place, and the next thing you knew, they were blowing the heads off large predators and laughing while doing it.

She should have been born a bear.

A lull in attackers made him hear her curse. "Stupid, cheap, made-in-China shit." She pitched the jammed pistol and pulled out a serrated knife.

Disbelief made him choke. "Do not tell me you intend to engage them in hand-to-hand combat. Are you insane? They have guns."

"Good point." She tossed the knife and began to strip.

"Um, Miranda, what are you doing?"

"Getting naked."

"I see that." Oh did he ever, and the sight was making him hard even given the situation. "I'm afraid to ask what for." Maybe one last quickie before they died?

"There's too many for me to fight in this form. I'm going to unleash my beast."

Great, she finally meant to escape. Or did she? "Are you going to get some help then?"

Vivid green eyes turned his way, and her lips quirked up on one side. "Why would I do that?" A sound in the hall made her turn away from him. "Don't worry. Me and my bunny will save you."

Ursa help him, she'd completely lost her mind.

"Miranda!" He shouted her name, but she'd already started to change shape, the bones in her body melting and reshaping, her skin sprouting silky white fur, and she got…bigger.

Chase's eyes almost bugged out of his head as he watched her go from curvy seductress to a thickly muscled, white-haired bunny with a giant cottontail and huge, floppy ears. But it wasn't until she turned and displayed foot long fangs that he laughed. And he laughed some more as the guards came pouring through the door, and Miranda—an honest-to-Ursa, saber-toothed rabbit—stomped on their asses while twitching her whiskers. She even stopped for the occasional nibble that resulted in piercing shrieks of terror.

Something about her primal shape and action called to his bestial side. A surge of adrenaline shot through him, dissolving the last of the drug. A moment later, his beast burst through his skin, a thousand pounds of pissed off—and somewhat aroused—grizzly.

Between the pair of them, they swept through the guards and their flimsy weapons, the occasional sting of a bullet making him roar in rage. However, it was the flamethrower that singed Miranda's fur that threw him off the edge, especially when she finally squealed in pain.

Hurt my fluffy bunny, will you?

The following moments were a red-tinged blur as he took care of the humans who dared hurt his Miranda. The idiot with the flamethrower screamed the loudest when Chase yanked off his arm and beat him with it. When that stopped being fun, he tore out his throat.

The battle was over in moments, leaving a pile of bodies and Chase standing over them, his body bristling and ready to inflict some more violence.

From up the hall, a two-legged humanoid lizard came jogging, its slitted yellow eyes taking in the scene of carnage. Chase roared a challenge, but the scaly-skinned being held up his hands and hissed, "I'm on your side. Where's Miranda?"

Chase whirled to see Miranda, back in her human shape, slumped to the floor. Blood covered her, but how much of it belonged to her and how much to the guards strewn about him, he couldn't tell. Her arm made him cringe with its bubbled skin and oozing sores.

Worry at her inert body made Chase lumber over to her to nudge her with his nose. Her eyes fluttered open, their green depths dull with pain. She tried to smile, but it emerged more of grimace. "I told you I'd get you free." Then her eyes rolled up in her head, and she passed out.

The lizard guy knelt beside him. "Shit. She must be hurt if she's not up and bouncing."

Chase grumbled in reply, an ache in his heart fueling his anger at those who'd hurt her.

"My fault. I never even guessed it was a trap. They somehow knew we were coming and planned to capture us all. Or so the rat that I caught confessed. They didn't count on Miranda or you, though, taking out half their mercs. Nice job."

Chase grunted. *A nice job would have resulted in Miranda not getting injured.*

"I'm Victor, by the way, Miranda's partner. Sorry we couldn't tell you about the operation. Orders from above, you know."

Operation? And orders from what? Just what in Ursa was going on? *Don't tell me Miranda is actually a real FUC agent?* The situation boggled the mind and screamed for some answers, but that would have to wait until he got his bunny to safety.

As if reading his mind, Victor said, "Listen, we need to get out of here before the human cops show up. Think you can clear the way while I carry her?"

Chase snorted then growled as Victor slid a hand under Miranda's naked body.

Slitted eyes turned his way. "Easy, man. She's like a sister to me."

Despite Victor's claim, Chase made sure to show a mouthful of sharp teeth as the agent scooped Miranda over his shoulder into a fireman pose, leaving one hand free to aim his gun.

"Let's get her out of here."

At least on that point, they agreed.

With Chase leading the way to take on stragglers, they made their way out of the basement, picking up other agents and the prisoner he recognized from earlier in his cell on the way. Oh, and a blanket to cover Miranda's naked ass because Chase had just discovered a new thing in his life he wasn't willing to share.

Chapter Eight

Fiery pain woke her, and for a moment, Miranda didn't know where she was. Well, she kind of knew—*naked and on someone's lap.* She rubbed her cheek against the nude chest she found herself against, the coarse hair on it abrading her skin. A rumble in said chest and a tightening of arms around her midsection clarified the situation.

Chase has me.

"Are you awake?"

"Define awake," she replied, lifting her head and looking around. The familiar back of the FUC van greeted her, along with Bo's white-toothed grin.

"Hey, if it isn't Bugs, back with the living. I didn't think there was anything that could take your furry ass down once you shifted."

Chase growled at Bo's statement, but Miranda chuckled and squirmed to sit upright. The sharp agony in her arm made her hiss in pain. "Damned flamethrower! Bullets I can handle, but fire bloody well hurts."

"You're insane," Chase muttered in a disgusted tone.

"But cute," she sassed back. And she knew he agreed judging by the tree branch poking at her backside. However, intriguing as she found his erect state, the pain of her injuries commanded her attention.

As Miranda scooted off Chase's lap, a sharp pain in her thigh made her drop to her knees on the floor. *Oops, forgot about that bullet hole.* While in her rabbit's berserker state, she tended to not feel injuries, but once the battle was done, talk about ouch.

The jacket covering her fell to the floor as she breathed through her pain. Not that she cared. Nudity didn't bother her. Most shifters didn't care, given how clothes had a tendency to shred when they shifted.

"Close your eyes," Chase growled. Miranda turned a startled glance his way, but realized he meant Bo, not her.

"I think I'll go sit up front with Vic." Bo moved away in a half crouch and clambered into the front, leaving Miranda alone with Chase.

"Whatever you think you're doing, stop before you pass out again," he growled.

"I'm fine now," she lied through gritted teeth as she scrounged for something to wear. They kept spare T-shirts and track pants, ugly brown FUC-issue, for emergencies such as this in the back. She tossed the largest ones she could find at Chase with her good arm. The burnt one…that one she kept tucked to her side and tried not to brush anything against it or move it.

It would heal. All her wounds would as a result of her shifter genes, but it would hurt like crazy in the meantime.

She heard Chase moving around behind her and wondered if she should turn around for a peek at his body before he covered it up. But given her current state, why tempt herself? She wasn't in any condition to do anything about it.

Holding back a sigh, she sat on her butt and tried to haul her pants on one-handed.

With a snort, Chase came to her aid. "Silly bunny." He handled her with care, sliding the cotton bottoms on, but he only pulled them past her knees before stopping.

"You've been shot," he said, his voice flat.

"Yup. It happens in my line of work sometimes. I'll take care of it when I get home. Now, are you going to finish pulling my pants on or what?"

"The fabric will stick to the wound."

"Probably, but I can't go inside with my bare ass hanging out."

A rumble made Chase's body vibrate, but he didn't say another word as he gently lifted her to tug her bottoms over her butt. He then took the T-shirt and popped her head through the hole in the top. Miranda slid her one arm through the cap sleeve, but hesitated to move the other. Any type of touch was sure to hurt.

Chase had a better solution. He grabbed the seam on the injured side and tore it right up to the neck. He then draped the folds over her back and chest, leaving her arm completely uncovered.

"We're almost home," he notified her as he lifted her back onto his lap, carefully cradling her in his arms.

Miranda couldn't deny her enjoyment at her spot in Chase's thick arms, although, she did make a token protest. "I'm fine." He just growled and tightened his grip around her less injured parts. She'd never known bears had such a protective instinct. *And I like it.*

The van rolled to a stop, and Victor turned around

in the driver's seat. "Home sweet home. Need a hand?"

"No." Chase barked out the word before Miranda could.

"Yeah, well, if you change your mind, Miranda's cell is programmed with a direct line to me and the FUC switchboard. As a precaution, I called ahead and got some guards stationed around your building. After I give my report, I'll be back to help keep an eye."

"Do you think they'll try again so soon?" she asked, worried that Chase might still be in danger.

"Doubtful, but then again, we didn't expect them to have this many mercs on their payroll hiding under our noses. Keep your eyes and ears peeled just in case."

"I'll keep her safe." Chase's promise sent a shiver through her—he sounded so deadly, and sexy. *But I'm the one who's supposed to be guarding here.*

Miranda opened her mouth to correct him, but, instead, sucked in a breath as Chase lifted her and, in a hunched walk, went out the back of the van. The jolting motion woke all of her injuries, and they throbbed painfully.

Thankfully, at this hour, somewhere after midnight but before dawn, there wasn't much traffic or humans around. Chase took her right to his lair—um, apartment—and settled her on the couch. He lumbered off, treating her to a view of his ass in too-tight track pants, not exactly the sexiest look, but the thought that he wore them underwearless made up for it.

He returned carrying a medical kit.

"I'm fine," she reiterated, lying through her teeth

because, at this point, the agony in her arm radiated in waves, counterpointed by the slow pulses of her two bullet wounds, one in her burnt arm and the other in her thigh.

"Good, then this won't hurt." He poured the disinfectant on the leg of her pants where blood stained the material.

She squealed, the fiery sting shocking. "Hey, I'm going to call the SPCA for cruelty to animals!" she exclaimed.

"Sue me. I know a great lawyer."

Humor? From Chase? She checked his head for signs of a bump.

"What are you doing?" he asked, exasperation coloring his tone.

"I'm checking for a concussion. You just cracked a joke, a sure sign of impending mental incapacity."

"Ha. Ha. Aren't you just the comedian?" Using a pair of scissors, he cut open her pants and exposed the jagged hole. "Did the bullet come out yet?"

Another fabulous shifter aspect. When their flesh healed, foreign objects tended to get pushed back out.

"Would you believe me if I said yes?" She batted her eyelashes hopefully.

He didn't reply, but handed her a folded facecloth. "Bite down on this."

"Why—" He stuffed the fabric in her mouth a second before he inserted some long tweezers in her wound.

Okay, bravery only went so far. Miranda screamed and bucked, her upper torso anyway. Chase held her leg steady with his free arm and body.

"Got it," he intoned in a soft voice. Miranda fluttered her eyes open, about to rebuke him for his calm demeanor, until she saw his face. Oh man, was he pissed. His eyes blazed. His mouth stretched into a taut line, and his jaw was locked.

"Why do you look like you're going to kill someone?"

Those ferocious eyes met hers. "Because I am."

Oh. Totally hot. So long as it's not me he's intending to murder because, at one point, I'm going to have to tell him what's going on and why he was taken.

He swathed on some antibiotic cream before bandaging the hole, which already showed signs of healing along the edges. In a day or so, it would be gone without even a scar as a reminder

He sat back on his heels and regarded her arm, her poor burnt and shot arm.

"Good thing I masturbate with my left, huh?" she joked.

The dark look he threw her appeared anything but amused. "Sorry, honey pie. This is going to hurt."

Thankfully, she passed out not long after he started pouring the disinfectant on her arm. When she woke, her entire right arm throbbed under its pristine white bandage.

"How long was I out?"

"Not long enough. I'm not done cleaning you up."

"The rest are just scratches," she protested. "Isn't it time we took a peek at yours? I know you've got a few holes in your hide."

"I can wait." His tone brooked no argument.

"Stubborn ol' bear," she grouched.

He wiped her face clean, dabbing at the one scratch on her forehead with ointment, his touch feather-light. She thought him done, but apparently, he'd catalogued the damage to her body better than she would have credited. He went on to the next wound, the hidden slice on her ribs, lifting her shirt, not high enough to bare any boob, but enough to make her heart race with the possibility. He dabbed some of the disinfectant on the ragged scratch, and she sucked in a breath, more because his fingers brushed the underside of her breast.

"You're all patched up, I think," he said, rising and stretching, the seams on the undersized shirt finally splitting, revealing patches of skin. "Unless I missed a spot."

"Yeah, you forgot something all right. What happened to my kiss to make it all better?"

His lips quirked. "You're one tough bunny. Anyone ever tell you that? Most females would be in hysterics right about now and in need of a slap."

"My mother always did say I was special," she said with a grin. "Of course, her exact term was hockey-helmet special."

Chase laughed, a deep, rumbly sound that made her join him. "What am I going to do with you?"

"Well, if you're not going to give me a kiss to make my booboos better, then sit your ass down. It's my turn to play Nurse Cottontail." When Chase went to sit, she halted him. "Yeah, I don't really trust myself with scissors around skin, so you might want to strip first."

Again, he flashed a smile at her, and darn it all, she found them addictive. However, his smile was nothing compared to the beauty of him when he used his two hands to rip the shredded remains of his shirt from his upper body. Oh, it was one thing to see him on the monitors, quite another to view him in the flesh.

Rippling muscles, slabs of them, defined pecs, a shag of hair that led down into a dark vee, and gaping bullet wounds.

"Good grief. How many times did you get shot?"

He peered down at himself. "I don't know, five or six times? They didn't hit anything vital, and the bullets have already popped out."

"You're acting awful nonchalant about getting shot. Shouldn't you be, like, freaking right about now?"

Chase shrugged. "I vacationed a lot in the Rockies. When hunting season hit, I used to get shot a lot."

"So that's why you're so well equipped? Medically, I mean," she added with a blush. "But I gotta ask, why allow yourself to get shot? Wouldn't it have been better to just not go around in your bear shape during hunting season?"

"It's easier to get honey when I'm my beast. The bees find it harder to sting."

Miranda blinked at him a few times before the laughter bubbled out. "Oh, you are a man of many layers, honey bear. Now sit down and let me pretend to help you."

"Fine," he said, plopping down on the couch, which creaked alarmingly. "You can clean the holes, but skip the bandages. I hate the way the tape rips out my hair when it comes off."

The visual he painted with his words set her off again into gales of laughter, and to her delight, he joined her.

When she finally sobered up, she set to work, not

that she had much to do other than swab his already healing holes.

While she cleaned, he finally asked her the question she'd expected. "So a saber-tooth bunny, huh? Can't say as I was expecting that. Actually, I don't think I've ever heard of one."

Miranda blushed. "It's a throwback in my line. Every other generation, we have some recessive gene that makes our animal shape revert to its more primitive form. My mom, a regular Bengal tiger, skipped it, but my grandma was a saber-tooth tiger."

"So you get your bunny gene…"

"From my dad."

Chase shook his head. "Okay, for some reason that's disturbing."

His remark miffed her. "Ah yes, I forgot you're Mr. I-don't-think-bunnies-should-mix-with-meat-eaters," she huffed indignantly.

"Call me old-fashioned, but I think, in a relationship, that it should be the man capable of carrying his mate around by the scruff of the neck and not the other way around."

"Oh. I guess I'm screwed then since I'm bigger than all the hares I know. Heck, when I'm shifted, I'm bigger than almost all the male shifters of any caste I know."

"You're not bigger than me."

"Gee, make a girl feel dainty why don't you?" She scowled. At his chagrined look, she laughed. "I'm pulling your leg. I'm not some old-fashioned damsel who's all hung up about her size and animal. And for your information, I know there are plenty of men out there who won't be intimidated by the fact I can kick their ass. I just need to find one."

"You didn't scare me," he said quietly, his eyes gazing into hers.

"No, I didn't, but as I recall, you weren't interested in me as a girlfriend because I was just a woodland creature."

"I changed my mind. I find it unbelievably hot that you're tough as nails with wicked long fangs."

"So who do you think would win in a wrestling match? My kick-ass bunny or your ferocious bear?"

Intent brown eyes tilted up to peer at her, and a slow, sexy grin crossed his face, transforming him from the staid and proper guy she'd gotten to know to drop-dead panty wetter. "Depends on the type of wrestling. Arm wrestling, I hate to admit, might be a close call, but if we're talking naked combat, then my sword would put me at a definite advantage."

She gaped at him, her cheeks blooming with embarrassment, but the heat from her face quickly transferred to her cleft as the look in his eyes turned smoldering.

And then he kissed her. Unlike his punishing embrace of before, and her light, teasing one, this one was about pure passion. The repressed desire of a man who was finally ready to lose control. Job or not, she intended to join him.

Of course, her body had other ideas.

"Ow! Ow! Ow!" She danced out of reach, her bandaged arm throbbing at the pressure she'd inadvertently placed on it.

His face turned ashen with chagrin. "Hold on. I've got something for the pain." He dashed off into his kitchen, and returned with a glass of water and some pills. "Sorry. I should have given those to you before."

"I don't like drugs," she managed to say through gritted teeth as she waited for the pulsing agony in her arm to die down.

"Take them, or I'll force feed them to you."

"You wouldn't dare!"

"Try me."

Somehow, she didn't think she'd win this battle. With a begrudging sigh, she took the pills and popped them in her mouth, washing them down with the offered water.

"Now lie down."

"I'm not tired," she grumbled, which turned out to be a lie because, all of a sudden, her eyelids grew incredibly heavy. "You drugged me," she accused before slumping on legs that would no longer hold her.

"I got you, my sweet honey pie," he whispered as he caught her in his arms. "Rest and get better. I won't let anyone hurt you."

Wait, wasn't that supposed to be my line? was her last thought before darkness sucked her down.

Chapter Nine

"What do you mean a fluffy bunny saved the bear?" The controlled voice rose in timbre until the peon who'd delivered the report abased itself, shivering in fear.

"It was a big rabbit, with fangs. Great big fangs."

"Rabbits don't have fangs, you imbecile. You should have waved a damned carrot at it." A lack of patience with the cringing rat made the order to dispose of him easy. Guards dragged the blubbering rodent away to the cages where they kept the test subjects.

"Boss." His lieutenant, a scurvy hyena, entered and waved a USB stick at him. "I think you need to see this."

"This better be good," was the reply. Impatient fingers drummed on the armrest.

The lackey, who'd managed to escape the ambush gone seriously wrong with only a few peons while losing all the test subjects plus the pricey mercenaries, popped the memory stick into a laptop, and moments later, a video played. Footage of the bear, slumped in chains, ran. Boring, that was until a female with platinum hair joined the captive, but it was what happened after the first wave of guards that proved most interesting.

Leaning forward with a jaw dropped, incredulity built as the unassuming female transformed into a creature of horror—and perfection.

"Who is she? I want her." *And the genes running through her body.*

"She's a FUC."

"Yes, she appears like a good time, but who is she?"

The hyena sighed, which earned him a dark glare. "A FUC as in agent for Furry United Coalition. She also happens to have the apartment across from the bear."

"And she's what, descended from killer rabbits?"

"No, even better. I did some digging. Her family seems to carry a recessive gene regressing some of the family member beasts to prehistoric times."

"I want her. Her and the bear, actually. He would be perfect for testing."

"As you wish." The minion who'd failed him, a damned hyena whose idea of hygiene made the gutter rats smell nice, scurried from the room with evident relief at having redeemed himself, thus saving him for one more day.

Alone once again, a smile burst forth as tiny hands rubbed together gleefully. A villainous chuckle would have been appropriate too, but mastery of the correct bone-chilling sound still remained out of reach despite all the practice.

But if I can harness that prehistoric gene, what I sound like won't matter. Finally, everyone will fear me, and I'll play whatever damned game I like, using them as balls.

Chapter Ten

Chase caught Miranda as she swooned, the painkillers acting as a sleeping agent, probably because they were meant for a guy his size and not hers. Keeping her injured arm in mind, he swept her into his arms and carried her into his room, placing her in his bed. The tattered remains of her clothing offended him and stank of blood and disinfectant, so he took a quick moment to gently rend them from her body, revealing absolute perfection.

He stood back to stare at her for a moment, knowing he should avert his gaze but unable to keep himself from drinking her in. As he'd noticed, she possessed perfect breasts, pillowy ones with large nipples that puckered as he watched. Her creamy flesh appeared silky smooth and complemented her rounded figure. The hair of her pubes—nicely trimmed into a heart—perfectly matched the platinum sheen on her head and surprised him because most women tended to keep themselves bare these days.

Having drunk an eyeful, and feeling slightly guilty about it, he drew a sheet up over her. Veering his attention from her delectable body, he mused over the events of the day. Questions tumbled in his mind about who she really was and what she knew about the kidnapping. But, even more pressing, the truth of his feelings for her fought to break free. The urge to sink himself in her body—permanently—remained present, but an odd need to protect her, to seek vengeance for her injuries, rode him even harder.

Just remembering the way she'd placed herself in danger to guard him against harm imbued him with warmth because he knew she cared, but it also flushed him with an icy-cold fear that she could have gotten killed. It also made him burn hot with anger that someone dared harm a silken hair on her head. *She's mine.* That claim kept repeating itself in his head, over and over. Worse, the more it bounced around in his mind, the more he wanted it to be true. He wanted Miranda, not just for one night or a few days, but a lifetime.

However, a new dilemma surfaced as it came to him that all the flirting and care she'd shown toward him might have been nothing more than a sham, a way to get close to him as part of her job. Victor had implied that Chase was an unknowing part of a secret operation of which Miranda had knowledge. Were the moments they'd shared together real?

Perhaps she felt nothing for him at all other than some lust—because even she couldn't fake the scent of passion.

Did he dare put himself on a limb when she could so carefully break it out from under him by telling him her actions were nothing more than an act because of some secret FUC operation?

The idea he might have fallen for her, fallen for a lie, should have angered him. Made him rampage. Sent him running for the honey. Instead, it bolstered his resolve.

Maybe I started out as a mission for her, but by Ursa, I refuse to believe that's all it is. Miranda cares for me.

And when she felt better, he'd test his theory by burying his cock in her, however many times it took, to make her say it aloud.

In the meantime, he hadn't gotten enough sleep, and a yawn made his jaw crack. Stripping first, because he hated to sleep in clothes, he crawled into bed beside her. He spooned her back into him, taking care not to jostle or put pressure on her injured arm. Her rounded buttocks fit into the curve of his groin with maddening perfection, something his wide-awake cock noticed. Splaying his hand across the smooth skin of her rounded tummy, he admonished his body to behave, but he didn't resist the impulse to place a soft kiss on the curve of her neck. She sighed in her sleep, and he smiled.

"My bunny," he whispered possessively before sleep took him down into its soft embrace.

****

Chase woke before she did, and after extricating himself carefully, he hit the bathroom for a shower and tooth brushing. Done, he peeked in to see her still sleeping, so he got some coffee going before he crawled back into bed. Nestling his body against hers, her back to his chest, her ass cradled against his dick, he placed light kisses along her neck as his hand stroked her belly.

She squirmed in her sleep, plastering her frame against him and arching her neck to give him greater access.

"Are you awake?" he whispered in her ear before nipping the lobe.

"Mmm, that depends. Will you promise not to stop if I am?"

He slid a hand up to cup a heavy breast, his thumb stroking over a nipple. "How's your arm feeling?"

"Itchy."

"And the bullet wound in your thigh?"

"Still needs a kiss, I think," she said, moving enough that she could flip onto her back. He kissed the impish smile on her face before rolling away to get up from the bed. "Where are you going?" she called out. He craned to peer at her over his shoulder and found her staring at his nude buttocks. "You know, there's got to be a law somewhere that says you can't just make a woman horny and walk away."

"It's called foreplay," he taunted. "Besides, you need a shower and some food." He turned back and continued to the bathroom.

"Is this your delicate way of saying I smell?"

Chase stopped in his tracks and whirled. He smirked when her jaw dropped at her frontal view of his body. "Honey pie, I want you in tip-top shape for what I have planned. And there's also the little matter of an explanation you still owe me."

"Yeah, about that—"

"Later. First, let's get you washed and take a look at your wounds. Wait here while I get the water warmed up."

It didn't surprise Chase to find her standing with a grimace when he returned, her hand vainly clutching at his sheet while not managing to cover a thing. With a cluck of his tongue and a shake of his head, he swept her up and carried her into his bathroom.

She peered about with wide eyes. "Good grief. Why is your bathroom so much bigger and nicer than mine?"

"I bought the apartment and renovated it to suit me." And nicely too, with grey slate floors, a tiled walk-in shower with multiple shower heads, and a granite countertop for his dual sinks.

"I didn't know you could do that."

Chase shrugged. "Apartments are just like a condo. Now enough about my awesome plumbing. Let's check you out." He sat her on the closed lid of the toilet and carefully peeled the bandage from her leg. The bullet hole had closed up overnight and, while still red and angry-looking, seemed well on its way to healing completely within the next day or so.

Tempting madness, he bent down and kissed the puckered skin. The scent and view of her bared pubes so close to where his mouth landed was an exercise in control.

"Almost all better," he said, lifting his head. She gazed down at him, her eyes bright.

He moved on to her arm next, unwinding the bandage from it and breathing an inaudible sigh of relief when he saw the burn reduced to dry, flaky skin. A shower would clear that dead flesh away and reveal the healed pink skin below. The second bullet wound had also healed nicely, and he kissed it, trying to ignore the way her heartrate increased every time he touched her.

"Looking good," he said, leaning back on his heel. "How's the pain?"

"Gone, but I think you forgot to check a spot." She grasped his hand and placed it on her tummy before dragging it up to her ribs.

Obliging her, he bent his head once more and ran his lips over the unblemished skin, the jagged scratch of the night before gone without a trace. That close to her breasts, though, the scent of her arousal swirled around him in a heady mix. He couldn't resist taking his path farther up. His mouth slid over the rounded curve of her breast and circled her nipple. He felt and heard her sharply indrawn breath as he teased the skin around her nub, its tight bud beckoning.

He pulled back.

She regarded him with heavy lidded eyes. "Mmm. Anyone ever tell you that you're an evil bear?"

"Only you're brave enough, apparently. Now, enough of your attempt to distract me. Get in the shower while I rustle up some breakfast and coffee."

She stood abruptly, which with him still in his kneeling position, put him eye level with a tasty-smelling pie. He allowed himself a deep inhalation before he stood, his body brushing up against her, the friction of her skin against his almost destroying his resolve to do the right thing.

"I hope you have some *sausage*," she sassed before pivoting and getting into the shower. Chase stared down at his jutting cock. *I've got sausage all right, honey pie, but by Ursa, I've got enough control that I can at least feed you first before you pass out.*

Chase knew from experience that their rapid healing abilities required copious amounts of food to sustain them. Much as he wanted to give in and make love to her, he feared more she would faint from overexertion and lack of energy.

He went back to the kitchen and started pulling things out of the fridge at random. His tasks were so noisy he almost missed her small cry of pain.

In a flash, he was back in the bathroom. "Miranda? What's wrong?"

"Nothing," she growled.

Chase sniffed. "Why do I smell blood?" He clambered into his large, tiled shower and saw Miranda leaning against the wall, her arm bleeding sluggishly.

"It's no big deal. When I was washing the skin off the burn, I felt something sticking out of my arm. I must have fallen on some glass last night and didn't notice it because of the scald mark."

"So you pulled it out yourself instead of calling me?"

She shrugged, and he sighed, stepping into the hot water so he could drag her toward him. She melted right into his embrace, her cheek pressing against his chest.

"What am I going to do with you?" he murmured against the top of her head.

She slid her arms around his body, and her hands cupped his buttocks. "I know what you can do. You're the one who keeps insisting we need to eat first."

"Miranda, I just want—"

Whatever he'd been about to say got lost as she dropped down to her knees, and in one unexpected motion, took him into her mouth.

Oh sweet Ursa. Chase could only gasp as she deep throated him, her lips sliding back and forth along the length of his shaft. She suctioned him tight, the pull of her mouth making his hips buck forward. He twined his hands in her hair, knowing he should push her away but unable to resist the incredible pleasure. And she enjoyed it too, the vixen, her contented rumbles vibrating around his shaft.

When she finally let go of him with a wet pop, to say, "Now, that's what I call a mouthful," he dragged her up and kissed her, his mouth hot and hard against hers. He anchored an arm around her waist and picked her right up so he wouldn't have to crane. She took that as an invitation to wrap her legs around his waist, trapping his jutting cock beneath her cleft.

Chase, lost in the pleasure of kissing her, leaned her up against the wall of the shower, his free hand sliding over the curve of her buttocks to her exposed sex. She keened into his mouth when he found her clit and rubbed it, his thick finger pressing against her sweet spot as their tongues meshed in a wet dance.

He slipped a finger into her pussy, and she trembled in his grasp. Back and forth, he seesawed his digit, the tight grip of her channel exquisite torture.

"Now, Chase," she gasped against his lips. "Please. I need you."

They were both too far gone for him to stop things now. He guided his cock to the entrance of her sex and, with a firm thrust, sheathed himself.

He almost spilled at the tightness of her, especially when she immediately began to shudder, the muscles in her sex contracting all around him. He shifted his grip so that both his hands held her buttocks while her back rested against the shower wall. Then he began to pump. In and out, he dipped his cock, sliding it out until only the tip rested at the entrance of her sex, and then he slammed it home, loving how she grunted and dug her nails into his shoulders. Again and again, he plowed her, the muscles of her channel tightening farther each time until, with a glorious scream of his name, she shattered.

The ripples of her orgasm milked his cock.

Exquisite pleasure engulfed him, but he held on to his own climax, determined to last a little longer. He stopped pulling his cock out as he thrust. Instead, he kept himself sheathed and kept pushing deeper, swirling his hips in a grinding motion, striking her inner G-spot. He could judge his success by how tightly her sex squeezed him, and exultation filled him when she screamed again as a second climax rolled over her.

Thank Ursa, because Chase could hold on no longer. With a yell of his own, he spilled his seed inside her, consciously not withdrawing, wanting to bathe her womb in his essence. Marking her. Claiming her.

She clung to him limply, her breath ragged, and as Chase came back to his senses, he felt ashamed that he'd allowed his lust to overcome his good sense. Never mind she'd started it; he'd known her still too weak. He quickly rinsed off the signs of their lovemaking and carried her out, right into the bedroom. He sat on the bed with her in his lap as he dried her off.

She mewled in pleasure, nuzzling the underside of his jaw, and pressing kisses against his neck.

"Stop that," he grumbled.

"Why?"

"Because, otherwise, I'm going to forget myself and plow you again."

"And the problem with that is?" she teased.

"You need to eat."

"Fine. I guess I can wait that long now that you've finally taken the edge off. But I'm telling you right now I know what I want for dessert."

Chase hid a smile as he hugged her to his chest.

Funny, he'd spent days agonizing over the reasons why he should not be with Miranda, and now that he'd had her, he kicked himself for fighting it. *Sometimes, I'm an idiot.*

Not trusting himself to keep his hands off if she remained nude, he loaned her one of his T-shirts, which hung on her baggily and hit her about mid-high.

It was the sexiest thing he'd ever seen, and he dragged her to him for a deep kiss that she responded to with feverish abandon. With a groan and a hard-on that could have hammered nails, he set her away from him.

"Kitchen. Now." Food, some answers, and then dessert. *I just hope she doesn't tell me anything that ruins that plan.* Not that he thought it would matter. As far as he was concerned, Miranda was his, and he'd deal with the consequences.

****

It was over lunch, a massive meal consisting of leftover pizza, fruit, a salad, buttered rolls, and, for some sweetness, frozen Nanaimo bars, that he finally asked her the question she dreaded. *Time to fess up and hope my lies haven't ruined what's burgeoning between us.*

"You work for FUC?" he tossed out nonchalantly.

"Yup. I'm one of their field agents, in charge of shifter security."

Chase leaned back on the couch and popped a cherry between his lips. He rolled the red fruit with an agility that made her cleft clench and distracted her.

"How?"

"Huh?" she asked, startled from her mental image

of his lips doing naughty things to her pie. He grinned as if knowing the train of her thoughts.

"How did you become an agent?"

"Actually, the first time I applied, they said no. Apparently, unless you've got some kind of tech or psych degree, they don't hire the smaller shifter castes. Something about sending prey to hunt predators. But then, I got jumped by a gang of hyenas who needed a lesson in the definition of no— "

"What?" Chase jumped up from the couch, and Miranda smirked.

"Calm down. My bunny took care of them, but in the process, my specialness came to FUC's attention, and I received an invitation to join."

"So that's where you learned to shoot?"

"Nah, my dad taught me that. He said he knew what it was like for people to underestimate him. In my case, he meant because I was a girl."

"Tell your dad thanks. I have to say, when you pulled out that gun, I was kind of worried."

Miranda grinned. "I'm a girl of many talents."

"That you are," he agreed, his smoky look making his meaning clear. Miranda foolishly hoped he'd leave things at that, but of course, he didn't. "So, what's this operation Victor was talking about? What does it have to do with me?" His eyes zeroed in on her. "And what exactly is your part in it?"

She couldn't hold his gaze. "Um, yeah, so I wanted to move closer to work, and what do you know? An apartment opened up that coincided with a new mission. One that involved watching over and protecting a bear."

"And exactly what do I need protection from?"

"Kidnappers and mad scientists."

He snorted. "You forgot crazy killer bunnies."

"Hey. Are you still offended my cute furry ass saved yours?"

"I'm offended that you thought I needed help in the first place."

"Says the bear who got caught in a trap made of his favorite honey buns."

"I was just about to break out when you showed up," he boasted.

"Break out in a sweat from the hallucinations maybe. It's okay, honey bear." She patted him on the cheek. "It'll be our little secret."

"What else have you hidden from me?" His eyes bored into hers.

With a sigh, Miranda told him about the list, and the missing/dead shifters. He said not a word during her recitation, but his face grew taut.

"So you were following me all this time?" He went silent, his face a placid mask, but she could see the wheels behind his eyes turning. It didn't bode well.

Miranda squirmed on the couch and forestalled answering by grabbing a handful of grapes and popping them into her mouth.

"Miranda?" His warning growl made her shiver.

She chewed faster and swallowed. "I already told you, I was tasked with protecting you."

"I got that part. But, after I was taken, it was hours before you guys came to get me, which means you didn't initially know I was even gone. So how did you pick up my trail?"

Damned lawyer. He just had to see the hole in her story. "I kind of also tagged you."

He crossed his arms over his impressive chest.

"Explain."

Miranda decided to show him. She stood up and walked over to him. "Bend your head forward." It took her a minute to find the tracker and peel it. Once she had it, she stood back and presented it to him.

"You chipped me?" His incredulous tone made her cringe.

"Hey, don't act so indignant. It's the only reason we found you in time. If we hadn't, you'd probably be drugged up in some lab getting shaved for experimentation."

"Anything else you'd care to share with me?"

"Not really if this is how you're going to act."

"Well excuse me if I have a problem being treated no better than an object. Is that all I was to you?"

Miranda didn't stop to wonder if it was the best idea or not. She just went with instinct and crawled onto his lap. To her pleasure, he didn't shove her off. "Would it help to know I wanted to tell you almost from the first moment I met you? You were never an object or just a job for me. I hated keeping my mission a secret from you."

"So no more secrets?" he asked, looping his arms around her.

"Nope. And I especially won't keep secret just how big your cock is. Woowee. Wait until the girls in the office hear. They are going to be so jealous of me."

"Miranda! You will not discuss my dick or anything else about me to anyone."

"Too late, sweet cheeks. As part of your security detail, cameras were installed in your apartment and at work. Unless they turned them off, which I highly doubt, FUC already knows we did the horizontal tango. Heck, Jessie probably had a pool going on how many times you could make me cum."

"What?" His roar that time definitely rattled some windows. "You've been spying on me?"

"Well, duh, wasn't that what we were just discussing?"

"You forgot to mention cameras."

"Sorry. Didn't even occur to me, as they're standard procedure."

"I'll standard procedure your asses in the Furry Alliance Court."

"The courts are the ones who set down our mandate and protocols, so go ahead. Be a baby bear about this." She stuck her tongue, and he growled.

"Woman, you are testing my patience." His grumpy face didn't turn her off, probably because of that insanity thing he kept accusing her of.

"And you're making me horny. Wanna fuck like bunnies?"

Her comment disarmed him completely, and he blinked at her. "You are completely and utterly whacked. You know that."

"Yeah. My mom says it's 'cause she dropped me on my head one too many times as a baby."

Chase's lips twitched, then trembled, then opened wide as he laughed. And laughed some more, the loud, rumbling sound so contagious she joined him. She turned to straddle him and tugged at his shirt.

"What are you doing?"

"Trying to get you naked."

"But the cameras?" he protested.

Sighing, she stood and stripped off her shirt. She used it to cover up the living room camera. "Happy now?"

Shaking his head, and mumbling about crazy, sexy bunnies, Chase stripped to reveal his magnificent body. She plastered herself against him, the skin-to-skin contact making her shiver deliciously.

"Now what?" he asked, lacing his hands around her body.

"Now you lie down." She loved the way he caught on quick. In moments, he lay flat on the floor, and she found herself perched on his bare, yet nicely hairy chest. She grinned down on him. "Perfect. You know, I've always wanted to boink on a bear rug."

"Miranda," he groaned.

"What? It's true." She tickled her fingers down his torso, following the bulging lines of his muscles and circling around his flat nipples. He tensed under her, his body rigid as he tried to rein in his desire. Like she'd let that happen.

She loved her ability to make Chase forget himself. To forget what she was. She especially loved the way his eyes glowed and regarded her with a possessive light.

Belonging to a man like him would probably feel pretty damned good.

She didn't have any illusions that, while he desired her for now, eventually, his lust for her would wane, and he'd recall bunnies and bears didn't mix—in his world at least.

But right this moment, naked and at her mercy, they were just a man and a woman. She planned to put that fact to good use. She swooped down to kiss him, her intended nibble turning into a full-blown, open-mouthed embrace where he raked his tongue across hers, pulling it into his mouth to suck.

A shudder wracked her body, a tremor repeated when his hands came about to cup her buttocks and squeeze, massaging her globes and making her moan. She squirmed on him, the moistness of her cleft making her slide on his belly.

"I want to taste you," he growled against her mouth.

"Right now?"

"I've waited long enough. Get your sweet pie up here." He didn't wait for her to move; he just used his bearish strength to drag her forward until she straddled his face.

And then, he showed her just what a bear's lips could do. First, he licked her, a long, wet swipe that made her shudder, especially since the length of his tongue surpassed anything she'd known, meaning he covered a lot of flesh at once. The tip of his tongue then circled around her sex, tracing her lips and her clit with an agility that made her mewl and then cry out as he delved into her pussy with a decadent stabbing of his tongue. All of that felt great, but she just about bucked off his face when his lips caught hold of her clit…and tortured her.

Dear God. Nothing on this earth could beat the sensation of his lips determined to drive her crazy.

Miranda clutched at his short hair as she rode his mouth, the intense pleasure of his lips tugging and stroking her nub making her keen aloud. She shattered, her orgasm hitting hard and fast as she found herself unable to hold back, the touch of his mouth too intense for her to handle.

And the evil bear, he chuckled against her sex, the vibration of it making her mewl then scream again as he thrust his tongue into her, lapping at her as if she were a tasty treat.

He built her pleasurable tension back up, holding her with his hands when she would have collapsed, his mouth devouring her until she panted for mercy.

"Please."

He took pity on her and slid her back down his body until she perched above his straining cock. Miranda sat herself on him, sheathing his length in one fluid moment that made his hips buck up and a grunt escape him. She, on the other hand, found relief in finally having something just the right length and size to clench around.

Hands splayed across his chest, she ground herself against him, her slow, languorous motion a form of torture of its own.

"Oh sweet Ursa," he gasped. "Don't stop."

She didn't. To her pleasure, the look on his face transcended the bliss he'd worn when eating. Actually, she'd never seen a man look so utterly happy, sexy, and tortured all at once. Then he opened his eyes and totally stole her breath.

Forget looking away or closing her eyes. She couldn't. Nor did she want to. His hands came to rest on her hips and helped her rock on him, and still she didn't break that intimate connection even as she felt her ecstasy approaching the brink again. She kept her gaze locked with his, wondering what he saw in her eyes. Wanting what she perceived in his. Needing it. The adoration, hunger, and possessiveness of his regard brought to her a height she'd never imagined, and when she crashed over it, in a quivering climax that he joined, she knew, in that moment, she loved him. Hopeless, and probably foolish, it didn't matter.

The fates help me, I love him.

Chapter Eleven

Chase woke alone in bed. Sated, and hearing the sound of her moving about his apartment, he didn't feel a need to track her down and drag her back—yet. He must have drowsed a bit because, the next thing he knew, she arrived at his side on stealthy feet. He expected her to climb back in for a cuddle or something a little more carnal. Instead, Miranda brushed his lips softly and moved away before he could rouse his lazy bear self to open an eye or snag her in his arms. Then, she left, the soft click of his apartment door a rousing bucket of cold water.

He sat up abruptly. *What the hell?* Maybe she'd gone to get some clothes or something. Make a call in to work and tell them she was spending the day in bed with him. Gone to get them some honey so he could lick it off her body.

A flash of white on the pillow beside him caught his attention, and he snatched up the note.

Dear Chase,

Last night was magnificent, but I know how you feel about the whole interspecies thing. I guess I shouldn't have taken advantage of you while you were vulnerable and still reeling from your near-death experience. What can I say other than I wanted you like a bear wants his honey? I thought it best I just leave with no messy goodbyes. I'm sorry at the havoc I've caused in your life, and even sorrier I failed in my task. I'll turn over the job of protecting you to someone better, who will protect you like you deserve.

Thanks for making me see stars,

M.

PS. After careful thought, I'd have to say I'm pretty sure my werebunny would beat your bear in an arm wrestling match any day.

Miranda was leaving him? After the night they'd just spent loving each other and doing incredibly dirty things? Yummy things that were even more addictive than pie. Chase shut his mouth before he drooled.

And she thought it was only a one-time thing?

Like hell.

Chase roared as he bounded out of bed and stomped across his apartment to his door. He flung it open and strode across the hall to pound on her door.

Miranda pulled it open with a surprised look. "Chase? What are you doing here?" Her eyes flicked up and down, widening as she took him in. "And what are you doing running around naked? Is this about the arm wrestling thing because if you want to challenge me, could it wait until after work? I'm running late."

Not a word crossed his lips, although he did grunt as he grabbed her and flipped her over his shoulder. He slammed her door shut before he stalked back to his apartment. Once inside his place, he whipped his portal closed as well. He set her down on her feet, ignoring her gaping mouth. Turning back to his door, he threw the deadbolt then, for good measure, he snapped the knob to unlock it right off.

Mission achieved, he rotated back to face her. She

looked him up and down, her eyes wide. "Oh my God. You've gone crazy. Did you bump your head during the fight with the bad guys? Or was I too late? Did they start experimenting on you before I saved your furry butt?"

"You left," he accused.

Her nose crinkled, and he found it adorable, which just reinforced her assertion he'd gone insane. "Well yeah, I left. I thought that's what you wanted."

"No. Yes. Not anymore. This wasn't how I'd planned the morning at all."

"Okay," she said slowly. "And just how was this morning supposed to go?"

"You were supposed to wake me up by rubbing your ass against my cock. I would have pushed you away because I'm a bear and I need lots of sleep. You would have ignored me, like you always do, and grabbed my dick to stroke it. I would have realized I could sleep later, and I would have flipped you onto your back and plowed you. After, we would have showered. You would have found an insatiable urge to give me head. Which I would have enjoyed, so much I would have picked you up and spun you on my cock for round two." Chase managed to say this with a straight face but a rock-hard dick, the first part of which surprised him. He never talked dirty. Just more proof she'd made him lose his mind.

Miranda peered at him incredulously and then burst out laughing. "I see you put a lot of thought into this. So, are you telling me you wanna boink one last time? Fine, we can have a quickie, but then I have to get to work."

"I want more than a quickie."

"Okay, you've totally lost me. I thought you'd be

happy I left before we had the fight where you told me this wouldn't work. Because the inconsiderate me would have then said it could, and then you would have yelled I was just a clingy bunny. So then I would have cried and said you were a big meanie before I went home to eat some carrot cake."

"You have carrot cake?" His tummy rumbled.

"I always have carrot cake with cream cheese icing, but you're changing the subject."

"You left."

She grinned. "Will it help if I said I didn't want to?"

He growled. "This isn't funny. Why don't you ever do what you're supposed to?"

A mischievous glint entered her eyes as she sashayed up to him, and he noticed for the first time what she wore. His shirt. She might have planned to say something else. Heck, she might have been about to give him the blowjob he wanted. He didn't care. The sight of her in his clothes hanging loose on her roused something primitive in him.

He didn't ask her permission. He didn't even give her warning. He just grabbed her and kissed her. Kissed her hard with all the urgency strumming through his body, imbuing his embrace with the things he couldn't say but felt. With the passion only she could inspire.

She kissed him back just as fervently, but he needed more than a taste of her lips. He needed to claim her, right that instant. Whirling her around, he placed a hand on her back and bent her upper body forward until she got the hint. With the scent of her arousal perfuming the air, she grabbed the back of the couch, thrusting her bottom out at him.

Sweet Ursa, she wore no panties under his shirt. Her pink sex gleamed already, moist and ready for him. Chase wasted no time, burying himself to the hilt in her velvety channel, claiming her with his body instead of words. And she took it, rocking her buttocks back against him, driving him deeper, her keening cries the sweetest sound.

It was fast, furious, and glorious. The need for foreplay unnecessary as their lust for each other made up for it. A pleasure so addictive, he didn't want to ever lose it. And most especially never share.

When he came in a hot spurt that bathed her womb, he drew her upper body back up and buried his face against her neck. Then he did something he'd heard about, something primitive but that seemed so right.

He bit her.

Not hard enough to take a chunk out, but with enough pressure to break skin and leave an impression of his teeth on her nape. He marked her, old style.

And she noticed.

"What the heck did you just do?" she squeaked, whipping around and slapping a hand to her neck.

"Nothing."

Her eyes narrowed. "Chase!"

"Would you believe I gave you an overly enthusiastic hickey?"

For a moment, he thought she'd question him more, but as usual, she never did as he expected. Instead, she laughed. "How did I ever think you prim and proper? You are a naughty, naughty bear, and if I didn't have to get to work, I'd stay and find out just how dirty you can get."

"So stay. I'll make it worth your while." He waggled his brows, and she giggled harder. He didn't understand what it was that made her laughter so addictive, but he enjoyed it too much to care.

"Can you hold that thought for later? That is, if you want me back later. Or is this where you finally give me the speech and I run off with a trembling lip trying to be brave?"

"You'll never let me live down the fact I thought bears shouldn't mix with bunnies, will you?"

She tapped her chin. "No, probably not. You can spank me for it later."

Oh, he would, but first, he needed to pay a visit to the FUC offices. Someone needed to do a little more explaining. And he wanted the original footage from the cameras watching his place. Chase wasn't about share his sex video with anyone, well, except for Miranda. Watching it with her would probably result in shared fun.

****

Sated again, Chase finally agreed to let her go to work, although, first, he needed to remove his broken deadbolt.

Miranda showered and dressed back at her place because even though Chase offered to wash her back, she wanted to get clean, not dirty again. Besides, she had some thinking to do. Her mind spun in circles trying to grasp what was going on with Chase. She'd thought he'd be happy she'd snuck out this morning. He was the one who'd originally said he didn't want to get involved with a bunny. So what happened?

It seemed, as with all things forbidden, they just couldn't stop themselves. They'd had sex, lots of mind-blowing sex. She'd assumed that, with his itch scratched, he'd want to rid himself of her.

Errr! Wrong. When he'd come stalking after her, naked, bristling, and utterly delicious, she'd just about declared her love for him. Which was nuts. How could she love an ornery bear who thought bunnies should frolic in the woods with the other small creatures? Of course, now that he'd met her other side, he knew her bunny didn't exactly belong with the vegetarians of her kind. Not when there was a chance she could eat them if her saber-tooth side got hungry.

It kind of tickled her that he liked her beast. Most guys either got intimidated or determined to prove she wasn't tougher than them. Chase just assumed he was, and treated her like a woman. His woman.

Which totally confused her. *Does he like me or not?*

Another surprise was he didn't seem to hold a grudge about the fact she'd failed to keep him safe. Nor did he seem overly pissed she'd, in a sense, lied to him about her mission and target. He seemed more concerned about her safety than his own.

What did make him blow up like an unstable WWII bomb was when she tried to let him off the hook. Disengage, so to speak. Most males would have sent her a thank-you card. Chase, instead, went all caveman on her, giving her a possessive hickey—which surprised the heck out of her. She'd not taken him for the mark-his-territory sort. If she didn't know better, she'd think he'd fallen in love with her. Nutsy, wishful thinking on her part, obviously. No way did her grumpy ol' bear, with strong notions of pure breeding, love her cotton-tailed self. Lust, yes, but love? *I wish.*

Caught up in her musings, she somehow hit a wall when she exited her apartment. She bounced back but didn't fall, as familiar paws reached out to steady her.

"Took you long enough," Chase grumbled.

She blinked up at him, wrinkling her nose. She'd kind of expected him to go back to bed once she left his place. After all, she'd interfered with his sleep. "What are you doing?"

"Walking with you to work. Shall we take the stairs?"

Her poor legs screamed in protest. They'd gotten quite the workout the last few days. "I was going to take the elev—"

He didn't wait for her to finish her sentence. He just scooped her up over his shoulder, Barbarian style, which made her skirt hike, offering him an unsexy view of her full bottom panties. Her poor cleft, so sensitized this morning, couldn't stand the feel of her usual g-string.

"Put me down."

"No," he answered in a reversal of roles that saw her trying to be the rational one. Chase, with a low whistle and bounce in his step, took the stairs by twos, jostling her. He held her firmly, though, his one arm tucked around her hip, his hand tucked between her thighs. Talk about distracting—and titillating.

Miranda tried to divert her attention from that big hand—the hand that knew how to wring screaming pleasure from her body. "I was really hoping you would hold off going to your office until I had a chance to get a new agent assigned to your case," she said.

"I don't need a new agent. I have you and Victor,

don't I?"

"But I failed to keep you safe," she sputtered as he jogged down the last few steps.

"You did your best with restricted resources, and when they dared take me, you got me back. I'd say you did a fine job. Besides, now that I know there's a plot to kidnap me, they won't be able to succeed that easily again."

She didn't understand this new Chase. He should be yelling at her. Grumpier than hell. Looking for honey. *Mmm, or spanking me for being bad.* Not excusing her and acting, well, all nice and stuff. "But—"

"Miranda, just leave it," he barked. She smiled. That was more like it.

Reaching the bottom of the stairs, he slid her off his shoulder and dragged her down his body before setting her on her feet. He didn't remove his hands, though, leaving them spanning her waist as he stared down at her.

"Keep in mind, just because I'm working a boring desk job now doesn't mean I don't know how to protect myself. Heck, when you fainted like a little girl, who do you think protected your furry tail?"

Miranda stuck her tongue out at him in reply, his reminder of her weakness embarrassing. She whirled and went to march out the stairwell, but Chase grabbed her and swirled her back.

"Don't I get a thank you for carrying you down all those stairs?"

She tapped her chin as if in thought. "I don't know. I mean, it's not like I asked you to," she said with a teasing smile.

"Nevertheless..." He picked her up and

thoroughly kissed her, melting her into a boneless mush that wanted nothing more than to march back upstairs to bed.

Why couldn't she again? Oh, right. Her job. *Oh shoot, my job, which I'm ignoring, yet again, because Chase is distracting me.*

She pushed away from him and shook her finger. "Stop doing that. How am I supposed to be on the lookout for bad guys if you make me forget my name?"

His slow, curving grin befuddled her almost as much as his kiss. "Really? I guess I should count myself lucky then that you remember mine when you come."

She glared at him. "As I recall, I screamed, 'Oh my God!'"

"Yes?" He looked at her serenely, but his eyes danced with mischief. She couldn't help herself; she laughed.

"You are incorrigible. But back to what I was saying. I need to be on the lookout for kidnappers, so no more kisses."

"First off, there isn't anyone capable of sneaking up on me when I'm in control of my senses. Secondly, I've decided I shall kiss you wherever and whenever I please."

"Says who?"

"Says me. I'm the man in this relationship. It's my prerogative to make decisions like that."

She gaped at him, not just in shock, but arousal. Say what you would, there was something hot about a take-charge man. "Since when are we in a relationship?" She held back the urge to bounce all over the place like a rubber ball at his claim. Talk about unexpected but awesome.

"Do I have to take you back upstairs and show you how it all started?" He waggled his brows suggestively.

"And they say I'm the crazy one."

"Apparently, you're contagious," he quipped as he snagged a hold of her hand and practically dragged her from the stairwell. She would have chastised him further, but she saw him sniffing the air and eyeing their surroundings, all his senses alert, doing her job. Dammit.

She spotted Victor a second after Chase did. Her crocodile friend, back in his human face, strolled up to meet them.

"About time you came down. I was about to go and see what was keeping you."

"Miranda was being obstinate," Chase announced.

"She does that a lot. I think it's a woodland creature trait."

"Must be. We omnivores are much more decisive," Chase added, his announcement agreed upon, or so she assumed by Victor's sage nod. "It must be because of their vegetarian diet."

"Um, hello, my bunny eats meat," she interjected.

"But do you still have giant floppy ears and a big, puffy tail?" Victor asked.

"Yeah, but—"

"Shhh, baby. Let the big boys talk." Chase winked at her.

Seriously? Miranda burst out into peals of laughter. "You guys are idiots. And I'm late for work. Victor, will you make sure Chase gets to his office safely?"

"Miranda." Chase's warning tone made her smirk. She hopped up and gave him a noisy kiss on the cheek before dashing off with a wave.

She hopped and skipped the few blocks to work, alternating between smiling and giggling. *I'm Chase's girlfriend.* The refrain played over and over in her head and drowned out any questions or doubts she had. She was a strong believer in if it was meant to be then things would work out.

Inside the FUC offices, there reigned a surprising calm with agents quietly going about their work. The war room gaped emptily, all the images and notes removed. *What the heck?*

Miranda hunted down Kloe, who appeared surprised to see her.

"What are you doing here?"

"I work here, remember?" Miranda answered with a roll of her eyes.

"Damn. And I'd wagered you wouldn't leave your bear's bed for at least another thirty-six hours."

"You guys were wagering on me?"

Kloe grinned, her eyes crinkling with her mirth. "Well, yeah, what else is there to do when we mostly cracked the case?"

Miranda squealed. "No way. What the heck happened during the two days I was out? Don't keep me in suspense. I want details."

Kloe caught her up to date. Apparently, while Miranda recuperated, among other things with Chase, FUC kept the human authorities away from the warehouse while they swept the basement for clues. While some of the shape-shifters had escaped the undercover location during their spur-of-the-moment rescue mission, they'd found enough information to locate other facilities. Simultaneous raids by other FUC offices had netted them even more info, and they had in their custody several shape-shifters involved in the kidnapping/experimentation organization. They'd also, in a coup, discovered and gained access to the off-shore accounts. *Ka-ching* for FUC, who always had to struggle for funds.

"What about the other missing victims?"

Sadness crept over Kloe's face. "Most of them were dead or dying. The few in the early stage of experimentation are in intensive care, but the doctors aren't very optimistic."

It chilled Miranda to know how close Chase had come to being one of those victims. "So, who was the mastermind behind it all?" Miranda asked.

At that, Kloe shrugged. "We never actually discovered that. Whoever it was hid their tracks well. Most of the lackeys never even met the one orchestrating events. Commands came down electronically. Although there is one male we've got agents on the lookout for. A hyena who was supposedly the right-hand man for the head guy."

"So Chase is safe?"

"As far as we can tell. Without money, troops, and labs, whoever it was won't be acting anytime soon, if ever. Good job, agent."

Miranda's smile held until she reached her cubicle. *Is it really over?* Somehow, it seemed too easy. Too neat. And the mastermind behind it all was still missing.

Why do I get the feeling this is only the beginning?

Chapter Twelve

Chase watched Miranda's retreating backside and followed, Victor at his side. Chase didn't question his need to do it, his need to see her safe. Besides, trailing her ass served more than one purpose—one, she'd lead him to the FUC offices, and two, that bunny had a serious wiggle to go with that delicious ass of hers.

"We need to talk," Victor offered after a few minutes of silence went by.

Chase almost snapped at him as it diverted his mind from the things he could do to a bared bunny's bum. "Talk about what?"

"Well, for one thing, I thought you'd like to know that the cameras in your place have been deactivated."

"I guess I won't need to file my motion to have them removed then. What about the footage?" Chase asked.

Victor handed over a USB key. "I copied all the recordings onto this and wiped the hard drives myself when done. I somehow didn't think you and Miranda would appreciate your video going viral."

Chase grunted a begrudging thanks. "You thought right. Thanks." He began to walk again before he lost sight of Miranda's backside.

"You're nothing at all like your brother," Victor added.

Chase stopped dead and turned to face the other male. "You know Mason?"

Victor nodded his head. "We served together before he left the unit."

"I never knew Mason was in the shifter army."

"Special forces," Victor corrected. "It's not something we brag about."

The knowledge that his carefree baby brother could belong to a group so serious, and deadly, shocked him. "Why did he retire?"

"Who says he did? The higher-ups had another use for him, just like they had a different use for me."

"Let me get this straight, you're working for FUC, but as an agent for the shifter government?"

"I am not at liberty to discuss current or past missions," Victor replied in a monotone.

"And Mason? Is that where he is right now? Off on some mission?"

A shrug lifted Victor's shoulders. "Who knows? That type of information would be classified. But forget your little brother for a minute; we have other things we need to talk about. Not here, out in the open, though. Can we go somewhere more private?"

Chase, watching the pert backside of his bunny entering some glass doors, frowned. "What's wrong with the FUC offices?"

"That's part of what we need to talk about. Don't worry. Miranda should be safe for the moment. No one will dare anything out in the open where the humans can see. And besides, that girl is tougher than most shifters put together."

"That she is," Chase replied with a partial grin. *And cute as a button too.*

They quickly made their way back to Chase's

office. Katy, his receptionist, took one look at their grim countenances and continued to type, her fingers flashing.

As soon as they closed the door, Victor told him the whole story about the list and the abductions. Most of it Chase already knew from Miranda, but it was the events that occurred after the rescue that made Chase's eyes widen. Victor related the tidy way things had fallen into place, but Chase got the impression something wasn't right. *Somehow, things seem...unfinished.*

"FUC seems to think everything's over," Victor said at the end of it all.

"But you don't?"

The croc shrugged. "I think what we raided and discovered was a facade. A visible trail to lull us into thinking we'd routed the problem. And what no one seems to want to recognize is whoever is in charge got information from the inside. Those guys in the basement holding facility knew we were coming."

"Could they have bugged the FUC offices or found out when they infiltrated the computer network?"

Victor shook his head. "The office is swept twice daily. As for the mission itself, we were off the radar, so to speak. With the computers down, we relayed the plan to reconnoiter the location and retrieve you only to the agents involved. And yet, they knew we were coming. There's only one conclusion. Someone inside FUC or closely associated to one of our team members is a traitor."

"And you let me send her in there?" Chase stood up, his voice a notch below a yell.

"Like I said, they won't dare try anything in there.

Not unless they're ready to blow their cover. Keep in mind, if they sent in a full-on assault, there's no way they could keep the humans ignorant. And we both know none of the clans or coalitions would stand for that."

The knowledge didn't soothe him. Seething, Chase sat down, the urge to fly to Miranda's side—to keep her safe—an almost desperate need. He focused his mind on a different portion of the puzzle. "Let's assume for a moment this whole thing isn't over. What was the purpose in the first place? Miranda said they were kidnapping shifters for experimentation. Anyone figure out why I and the others were chosen?"

A pensive look dropped over Victor's face. "No one could come to a consensus on that. None of you shared an animal, but what you all had in common was size and strength. The few bodies found showed signs of mutating those two features by either radically reducing or increasing it."

"Someone trying to enhance or detract from the shifter gene? That sounds almost military to me. Are we sure the humans aren't involved?"

Again, the croc lifted his shoulders. "The agents in place in the various human government and military agencies haven't heard or seen a thing, so they can't be counted out. But, given some of the minions of this criminal are shifters themselves, I'd wager a guess it's either a shifter or someone in another species group masterminding it all."

Chase rubbed his chin. "Maybe trying to make a super army of shifters. Taking the strongest males and trying to make them stronger while discovering ways of making the opposition weaker."

"That was my thought until we got our hands on some new information during the raids. See, we thought it was only men snagged, and the list we acquired seemed to support that theory. However, we found a second smaller list when routing through their breached network, a list of women who all had size and strength when in their beast form as a denominator."

An icy chill went through Chase. "Was Miranda on that list?"

"No, but not too many people know about her other side. It's not something she advertises or resorts to often. Heck, I think in the office, currently only me, Jessie, and Kloe have ever seen her as her giant wererabbit self."

Chase heard the but in his words. "But now that the traitor knows about her saber side, you think she might have a target on her." Victor nodded, and Chase mused aloud. "And if this mad scientist, or whoever he is, just lays low while the smoke clears, he might come after her next."

"I could be wrong," Victor said.

Somehow, Chase didn't think so. His gut told him that Miranda was in danger. "So what do we do?"

"You could hide…"

"And live life constantly looking over my shoulder making sure she's not in danger? No thanks."

"Then the only alternative is—"

"Use me as bait!" Miranda bounded into the room with a loud exclamation, and Chase just about fell off his chair.

"Miranda! What are you doing sneaking around like that?" he bellowed.

"Hey, you're the guy who claimed no one could sneak up on you." She smirked.

That only worked if he wasn't already covered in the luscious scent of the one sneaking, though. "I'm going to put a bell on you," he growled.

"You'd have to catch me first," she taunted.

Victor folded his hands and shook his head. "How long have you been listening?"

"Long enough. So, how cool is that? A mad scientist might want me for some freak experimentation. So, when do we launch the trap with me as tasty bait?" Excitement lit her face and made her glow. The only saving grace about her rapt expression was she glowed more when he made love to her.

"Victor, could you give Miranda and me a moment alone?"

The croc grinned. "Good luck. You know she's not going to change her mind, right?"

Miranda beamed. "My partner knows me so well."

Chase growled, the rumble getting louder and louder. "This is not a game," he shouted.

"I know," she sassed back. "Hello, in case you haven't noticed, this is my job."

"I don't like it. You could get hurt."

"Why, are you planning on not protecting me?" She batted her lashes at him.

He groaned and rubbed his face with his hands. "Of course I'm going to protect your furry, hare-brained ass. That's not the point. I care about you, and the idea that someone might want to hurt you makes me want to—"

"Have angry sex?"

"No, it makes me want to—"

"Have make-up sex?"

"No. Would you let me finish? It makes me want to—"

"I know, kill something."

Chase sighed and buried his visage in his hands. "I need some honey."

"Oh."

"So that I can slather it all over you and have honey sex."

Miranda's laughter pealed out, and Chase grudgingly joined her. "Listen, are you sure you want to try this? There's no guarantee this guy and his goons will come after you."

Bouncing around his desk, she hopped into his lap. "Careful, my grumpy ol' bear. If you don't stop acting so nice, I might start to think you actually like me."

"And if I did?"

Her eyes widened, but before she could reply, Victor came back in. "Sorry to interrupt, but I figured better now than when you got all naked and stuff. I've got to get back to work. Listen, it will probably take a few days at the very least for the perp to get organized enough to try something. Why don't you both take off for the weekend? I've got a cabin up in the woods you can use."

Miranda squealed and jumped up to hug Victor. While she hugged the other male—which made Chase suddenly want to tear off his head and throw it at something—Victor sent him a pointed look and mouthed, "Don't tell her."

Chase got it. This cabin was a ploy to lure the traitor out. And he didn't want Miranda to know, probably for fear she'd mention their plan to use her as bait to whoever the FUC traitor was.

Great. He'd get her all to himself and would somehow have to keep his mind alert for danger while she did her best to make him lose his mind with the things her body—and her mouth—could do.

Life was so much easier when all he had to look forward to was his next spoonful of honey. *But definitely not as much fun.*

Chapter Thirteen

The sense that something was up nagged Miranda the whole time she and Chase packed. She felt it in his frantic lovemaking—at her place, finally—on her bed, where, trapping her under his big body, he pounded her as if desperate to make every thrust count. She quite enjoyed the wildness of it, but it made her realize something.

Chase is afraid—for me. And she didn't quite know how to handle that. Miranda usually looked after herself. It's what her parents had taught her even before they found out her bunny side had big, sharp fangs. Odder, Chase knew firsthand she could defend herself, and yet, now more than ever, he acted as if he was the one in charge of guarding her—talk about role reversal.

She tried to broach it with him and got so far as, "Hey, crazy bear, paranoid much?" before he grabbed her and silenced her with a kiss. Liking that game, she threw out more comments until with a growled, "Miranda!" she got what she deserved, a hard pounding bent over the couch.

His anxiety didn't lessen, even once they got into his car, a large, dark sedan with the most comfortable seats ever. He appeared on high alert, his eyes continually scanning all about them. The novelty of having someone looking out for her, though, quickly wore off.

She waited until they were on the highway to pounce. "So, what plan did you and Victor concoct?"

His grip on the steering wheel tightened, but he didn't look at her when he casually replied, "What are you talking about? We're just going on a relaxing weekend."

"Oh please. There is nothing relaxing about what you and I do. Although it sure does leave my muscles feeling mushy." She squeezed his thigh as she said this, and he finally glanced in her direction, his eyes blazing with arousal.

"Be a good bunny, or I won't let you have any of the treat I bought you."

"A treat?" She bounced in her seat. "What did you get me?"

"Be a good girl and you'll find out when we get to the cabin."

"Oh, I know how to be good," she purred. Slipping out of her seatbelt, she leaned over the console and her hands worked at unzipping his pants.

"Miranda!" he yelled with a tone she rapidly thought of as endearing. "What are you doing?"

"What I do best," she sassed, freeing his cock. His breath sucked in as she stroked her hand up and down his already burgeoning length.

"How am I supposed to—Ahhh…" His rebuke died off into a groan of pleasure as she took him into her mouth, engulfing more than half his length. There was just too much of him to go all the way to the root, but she solved that problem by using her hand to grip his base, fisting him in time to the up and down motion of her mouth.

"Sweet Ursa," he moaned. "You're going to kill us both."

She slurped her way up to the top of his dick before answering. "Think of this as extreme distraction training. A prepping, so to speak, for when we're all alone in that cabin, boinking like wild animals, never knowing when company might drop in." Before he could form a coherent response, she slid her lips down his length again, her teeth grazing along his skin.

The way he pulsed in her mouth, the taste of his pre-cum, and his low rumbles of pleasure all combined to arouse her—and without a single touch by him. What was it about Chase that made everything about him a delight?

Is it the fact I love him?

Not something she dared say aloud, but she showed him, sucking him with hollowed cheeks, bringing him to the brink of pleasure, and then helping him over it. The car swerved as he climaxed, and she swallowed his pleasure, her own cleft spasming in a mini release of its own.

When she finally sat back in her seat, a grin on her face, he turned his head to pin her with a smoky gaze.

"Bad bunny."

"I thought I was rather good myself," she replied with a lick of her lips.

He couldn't stop his mouth from twitching. "You do know I'm going to make you pay for that, right?"

"I look forward to it. The sooner, the better. These wet panties are mighty uncomfortable."

Her peals of laughter filled the sedan as her bear put the pedal to the metal, cutting their trip considerably.

The cabin Victor sent them to defined the word

rustic. Imagine an hour on a dirt track, where tree branches scraped the side of the car as they fought to close the world's ability to breach them. They wound their way up the sinuous path of the mountain, leaving civilization—and bakeries—behind.

The remoteness appealed to Miranda, and she clapped her hands in delight at her first view of the cabin. Built of roughhewn logs, weathered from the elements, it sported a wide, inviting porch, a shingled roof, and a tire swing.

As soon as the sedan slid to a stop, she scrambled out of the car and hopped over to perch herself on the rubber tire hanging from the rope. She screamed, "Wheee!" as she swung dizzily in the air.

A grin crossed her face as she saw Chase standing a few feet away, watching her while shaking his head with an expression of disbelief.

"Wanna turn?" she offered as she tilted her body to sway his way.

"Actually, I do," he replied, his big hands flashing out to grab the swing, halting its momentum. His eyes holding hers, she felt his hand fumble at her shorts. With a growl of impatience when they wouldn't come free, he tore them from her body, along with her panties.

Moisture immediately pooled in her sex. How could it not with his heated intent warming her body? His fingers found her slick opening, and he inserted a digit, coating it in her body's lube before withdrawing it to run it over her clit.

Miranda, her hands still clutching the rope of the swing, moaned as she spread her legs wider. He fitted his body between, his stroking fingers leaving her for a moment to fumble at the closures of his pants. A moment later, contact returned as he rubbed the swollen head of his dick along her pussy, pressing it against her clit.

"Kiss me," he ordered.

Miranda leaned forward, her lips finding his and opening for the thrust of his tongue. While he kissed her like a man starving, he slid his cock into her sex, his thickness stretching her and making her pelvic walls cling to him tight. She found herself swaying as he used her perch on the swing to move her body back and forth, driving his prick in and out of her.

Miranda moaned and then yelled as he put more force in his movements, her suspended position allowing him to slam her onto his shaft, so nice and deep that it hit her G-spot. Over and over, he pounded her until her body, with a final clench, orgasmed. As her pussy spasmed around him, she screamed, "Oh my God."

He hissed, "Yes!" and then drove into her one last time, the heat of his seed bathing her.

Boneless with satiation, she almost fell out of the tire swing, but Chase was there to catch her. She clung to him as he carried her into the cabin.

"Mmm, that was fantastic," she purred in his ear. "Can we do it again tomorrow?"

"Probably not."

She growled and nipped his lobe. "Why? I liked it. You liked it. Or did you have some even more perverted outdoor fun for us to try?"

Chase set her down on the plaid-covered couch. "No more outdoor sex for now. Victor and the others should be arriving right about now," he said, glancing at his watch.

"Aha!" she yelled, bouncing up. "I knew you had

some secret plan brewing. Are you going to tell me about it now?"

He eyed her up and down, his gaze lingering on her denuded crotch. "Make me."

Miranda stuck her tongue out at him. "You wish, you dirty ol' bear. Besides, I'm not hungry anymore."

"We'll see about that." He whirled on his heel and went back outside. Miranda didn't bother fighting her curiosity. She watched from the window as he went to the trunk of his car and, after opening it, pulled out a large box. He returned to the cabin and set his package on the table. From the open top, he pulled out a plastic container. Approaching her, he waved it under her nose.

Said nose twitched, and her mouth watered. "Is that carrot cake?" she asked, fighting an urge to check for drool.

"Yup. Freshly baked with extra cream cheese icing."

She dove on it, but he held it out of reach. "I don't know. You were a pretty bad bunny on the way up."

"Tell me what you want," she begged. "I'll do anything for carrot cake, you evil bear."

"Anything?" he asked with a waggle of his brows.

"Why do I get the impression this is a trick question?" she grumbled.

"Would I use your weakness for carrot cake against you?" he asked with a patently fake innocent expression.

"Yes. Now name your terms."

"No wandering around outside alone."

"Fine, but you better be prepared to keep me entertained then."

"Oh, I've got plans for that. Number two, no letting anyone into the cabin unless it's me or Victor."

"Why? Are you planning on leaving? And besides, who knows we're here?"

He ignored her question. "Are we agreed?"

"If I do, do I get the cake?"

He nodded.

"Hand it over then."

"Why don't I cut us both a piece?"

Miranda shot him a glare. "You want me to share my carrot cake?"

"Come on, just a little piece."

"Fine. I'll share with you and only you, but that's just because I love you." Miranda slapped a hand over her mouth.

A stunned look crossed his face, and his jaw dropped. "What did you say?"

"Nothing. Let's find some plates."

****

Nothing indeed. Chase watched Miranda's bare bottom as she scrounged through the cupboards looking for plates and cutlery.

She loves me.

He wanted to beat his chest and roar it to the world. Pick her up and twirl her in circles until she drowned him in her giggles. Tell her that, as far as he was concerned, she was better than honey, and he loved her too.

However, while she was stuffing her face with cake probably wasn't the most opportune moment to make that kind of declaration. But before the weekend ended, one delectable bunny with impressive teeth, and the cutest button nose, would know that he, Chase Brownsmith, irritable bear and lawyer, loved every crazy inch of her.

Over the carrot cake, where she sliced him a tiny piece in comparison to hers, she blurted out her question again.

"What is going on? And don't tell me nothing, or else I'll tie my legs together and cut off your honey."

"You could try, but I'd chew through the rope," he warned. "But I was planning to tell you anyway once we got here. We're trying to set a trap."

"We being you and Victor?"

"Yup."

"So why not tell me in advance? I can help, you know," she said, her tone and look highly offended.

"I know you can help, but I wanted everyone in the FUC office to think this truly was a vacation."

"You think there's a spy in my office?" Her forkful of cake didn't make it into her mouth and hovered just in front of it.

He leaned forward and sucked it off.

"Hey," she exclaimed, jabbing her fork at him. "Give that back."

"Come and get it," he dared, leaning back and opening his mouth.

"Evil bear," she muttered. "So we have a spy in the office, do we? That explains a lot. Which means this trip is a trap, with Victor hoping to flush the spy out by using us both as bait. I wish I'd known. I would have packed more than one knife and gun."

"You packed weapons for a weekend tryst?"

"Well duh. There are mountain lions, crocodiles, and ornery bears in these parts, apparently." She snorted.

"You forgot killer squirrels."

"Ha. Ha. Aren't you just a scream? See if I protect you now, Mr. Smartass. And just what did you bring to this ambush? Huh?"

Chase leaned back and grinned at her slowly. "Me."

"That's it?"

"Yup. I'm more of a hands-on kind of guy."

"Hmm. You know what? I like how you think. Care to show me just how those hands of yours work?" She winked, and in a flash, he chased her all over the cabin with her squealing and hopping. When he finally caught his breathless rabbit, she smiled so sweetly at him that his teeth ached along with his heart.

It seemed the perfect moment to declare his affection for her irritating person, but she literally grabbed a bear by the balls, and well, the only thing he managed for a while after that was incoherent moans.

When they finally lay spooned in each other's arms, her even breathing fluttering against his chest, he brushed his lips across her forehead, his heart so full of affection for this woman that it scared him. And elated him.

I love you, Miranda.

Chapter Fourteen

The birds woke her, their energetic chirping breaking through her slumber. She found herself wrapped in Chase's arms while lying on his chest. An interesting position for sure. She couldn't resist studying him in his sleep from his shadowed jaw to the dark lashes fluttering against his cheeks.

Such a handsome male and, for the moment, all hers. She'd felt a moment's panic the day before when she accidentally blurted out she loved him. Nothing like declaring affection to get a male running, but thankfully, Chase had overlooked her wayward words.

Or they didn't bother him.

She couldn't deny that he no longer seemed to find her a pain in the ass anymore. On the contrary, he'd turned over a new leaf and now teased her back just as much. She doubted she'd cured his dour disposition, but at least around her, he'd lightened up. Surely that counted for something?

And he did say we're in a relationship. Which meant he expected what they had to last longer than a few days. However, she'd better not get her hopes up about anything permanent. Nothing would change the fact that she was a bunny.

With a sigh, she extricated herself from his grip. He grumbled in his sleep and opened one sleepy eye.

She kissed his chin and whispered, "Go back to

sleep. I'm going to shower."

Grunting, he drifted off again, and she wandered off to take care of her bladder. She then cursed Victor's hot water system as she washed under tepid water. Clean, she dressed in one of Chase's shirts and a pair of her undies.

While drinking a cup of coffee, she peered out the front cabin window, entranced by the truly beautiful setting. A flash of movement in the woods, at the edge of the clearing in front of the cabin, made her frown.

Victor was never so careless. Shooting a look over her shoulder in the direction of the bedroom, she gnawed her lip. She'd promised not to leave the cabin. But surely, the porch didn't count. She'd leave the door open so Chase could hear her.

It occurred to her to grab her gun or knife in the bedroom, but if she did, Chase would surely wake. Then he'd ask her what she was doing, then he'd run off all testosterone pumped, and she'd never get her morning sex. On second thought, better to just check things our surreptitiously on her own.

Slipping the door open as silently as possible, she wandered outside and sat on the first step, her coffee mug cradled in her hands. She pretended to be lost in thought, but in truth, her eyes tracked the periphery of the yard.

It shouldn't have surprised her so much to see Frank stepping from the woods, but it did make her sad. She would have never guessed he'd turn traitor.

"You might have a hard time huffing and puffing this house down," she joked weakly.

"Sorry, Miranda. But you know how it is."

"No, I don't, Frank. I thought we were friends."

He snorted. "There are no friends when you owe money to the vampire bookies. I'm the big, bad wolf, rabbit. Didn't you ever read your fairy tales?"

"Yeah, and as I recall, the wolf always loses." Miranda set her cup aside and stood. "Give yourself up, Frank. Don't make this harder than it has to be."

Braying laughter escaped him. "I'm in too deep to back down now."

"And I'm not alone," she reminded him.

"Already taken care of."

Miranda frowned then blanched as comprehension hit. "Chase!" she yelled, whirling to run back in the cabin.

Arms wrapped around her from behind, and she felt a pinprick in her arm.

"Say goodnight," Frank whispered.

"Screw you," she muttered instead, and before Frank could depress the plunger, she burst out of her skin and clothes. People, cocky males in particular, always underestimated her, which worked to her advantage.

With a twitch of her nose, she grabbed Frank's arm—with paws that still held a slight resemblance to hands with stubby, furry fingers—and swatted away the threatening needle. She bent it back then back some more until she heard a snap and a scream. Oops.

She turned and surveyed her former friend kneeling on the ground, his useless arm dangling.

"Bitch, that fucking hurt."

Unable to reply with words, Miranda instead gnashed her teeth. Frank squeaked and scrambled backward on the porch, hollering for help. She pounced on him, cutting his cry short as something important cracked in his body. Too late.

From around the house and the woods poured camouflage-clad bodies. Not as many as in the basement she'd rescued Chase from, but enough to prove worrisome, especially when she saw them loaded with dart guns and Tasers.

"Take her alive," was the yelled command by a butt-ugly male who stood behind as his minions came charging at her. Miranda hopped off the porch, determined to bring the fight to them. She almost stumbled, though, when a roar shook the cabin behind her, and then she tried to grin as a huge, really pissed-off grizzly came charging through the door, his momentum smashing it against the wall.

Would you look a that? Apparently, the plan to subdue Chase didn't work out so well.

But still, it was only the two of them against a whole bunch of armed humans. She began swiping at the nearest bad guys with her fluffy paws, evening the odds, when, from the woods, Victor came jogging, firing with unerring accuracy—silver bullets to the brain. Ouch. That was one injury no shifter or human could heal from.

As she battled the startled combatants, she also caught sight of Bo and Kloe, who also resorted to weaponry instead of their shifter selves. It gladdened her to see that those she truly counted as friends hadn't betrayed her as well.

The tide of the battle turned quickly in their favor, and she found herself chasing down her prey, who kept trying to back away so they could take aim and fire. What a mistake for them. It just made them easier targets for Victor and the gang to pick off. Diverting her attention from the battle, she searched for her love.

Catching a glimpse of Chase bearing down on a scurrying and screaming ratman, she wanted to grin. *He is right. He's the only weapon he needs.*

The chaos around her subsided with the number of adversaries dwindling to single digits, and she'd just decided to make her way over to Chase when a zinging pain hit her in the hip. The Taser sent volts of electricity running through her. Not a big deal until the second, third, then fourth one hit. Hot damn, that hurt.

Miranda hit the ground, her body convulsing. She lost hold of her beast in the excruciating pain of the energy jolt, not that she had time to appreciate how she must look jittering naked on the ground like a bug on a griddle.

But she did hear Chase's roar of rage.

****

Chase heard Miranda's scream of pain first, but by the time he'd disposed of the fox shifter in his grasp and turned, she'd hit the ground. In her human shape, she writhed on the ground in evident agony. The sound of fury that emerged from his mouth almost shook the ground. The male orchestrating the events, a hyena by scent, didn't even flinch as Chase went tearing across the yard, trampling the prone bodies underfoot. The hyena—who'd signed his death warrant when he hurt Miranda—threw himself at her naked form and scooped her up.

Chase skidded to a halt when he saw the blade at her throat.

Her body still shook with the residue of the Taser strike, her involuntary shudders pressing the point of the knife into her skin and causing a red streak to come rolling down.

It took only a moment's thought to reshape himself, but even in his man body, he retained his primitive anger. "Let her go and I might let you live," Chase growled.

Laughter, tinged with hysteria and madness, came sputtering out of the hyena shifter. "I'm dead if I go back without her. The master doesn't take kindly to failure."

"You can't have my mate," Chase shouted, frustration and fear making him irrational.

"How archaic," the hyena said with an arched brow.

"I think it's sweet," Miranda mumbled before she rammed her elbow back as her foot jammed down on her captor's foot.

The hyena male jerked, the blade slicing at her neck, but Miranda didn't seem to notice the pouring blood as she twisted in his grasp and, in some kind of martial arts move, flipped him onto his back. Before she could kneel on his chest—naked—Chase arrived and took him from her. Lifting him up, he shook the stunned male, rage controlling him.

"Who the fuck sent you to do this?" Chase yelled.

"My master feared I might get captured." The hyena grinned at him, a sickly, not quite sane smile that made Chase almost shiver.

"Who is your master?" Miranda asked, sliding up beside Chase.

"My master had a message for you. Said to tell you that the meek shall inherit the earth, and then rule it."

"How original," Chase drawled. "Sounds like your master must have small balls sending everyone else to do his dirty work."

"If you only knew," muttered the hyena. "Don't worry. You'll meet my master eventually. As for me, this is goodbye."

Chase went to ask the male how he thought he was going to escape when the shifter's eyes rolled up in his head and his body began to shake.

When the froth started to spill from the hyena's blue lips, Chase tossed his body away and then turned to Miranda, who suddenly clung to his freed arm.

"I think I need a Band-Aid," she murmured before slumping.

Chase caught her in his arms and carried her back toward the cabin.

Victor caught up to him. "I think we got them all. What happened to the hyena?"

"He's dead. Some kind of poison or suicide pill. I don't know. He didn't say much before he kicked the bucket."

"What's wrong with Miranda?"

"She's hurt," Chase growled. "Now get out of my way before you join her."

Chase closed off the sound of Victor's chuckles by slamming the cabin door shut, worry over Miranda the only reason he didn't slam his fist in the croc's face.

"Oh good, are we alone?" she whispered.

"Just hold on, honey pie. I'll get you bandaged up in a second."

"Bah, 'tis but a flesh wound," she scoffed in a bad Monty Python impression. "Although, I could use a shower."

Letting her down, Chase glared at her. "You

mean you were faking lying on death's door?"

"Well duh," she replied, rolling her eyes. "If I hadn't, we'd be out there helping the cleanup crew instead of in here about to indulge in some serious interspecies sex."

"I love you," he announced. "You crazy, rascally rabbit. You drive me freaking mental. You make me want to gag you at times, mostly with my cock. And you make me want to kill everything that looks at you, but dammit, despite it all and the fact that you're a vicious woodland creature, I love you."

Tears brimmed in her eyes, appalling him. "That's the most beautiful thing anyone has ever said to me," she sniffled. "I love you too, you big ol' bear. Even if you're grumpy and my bunny is stronger than your bear."

"Is not."

"Is too.

"Is not."

"Oh yeah?" she said slyly, a mischievous look in her eye. "Prove it."

He did—in the shower, where he held her up for a spin on his cock. In bed, where he held her down as he tortured her pussy, and then again, when he wrestled her for the last piece of carrot cake—which he ended up sharing.

Love could make a bear do crazy things, apparently.

Epilogue

A week later…

Chase woke up to a strange noise and noticed, that while the spot beside him still oozed warmth, it didn't hold a certain naked body. *What's my bunny up to now?* No strange scents assailed him, although a familiar odor caught his attention, even if he couldn't place it.

The odd sound that woke him approached, and Chase recognized it as someone choking. Jumping up from bed, his eyes flew open, and he found…Miranda, shifted into her deadly bunny, and hugged in her massive furry arms an intruder dressed from head to toe in black.

Chase took a big sniff and snorted. "It's okay, honey pie. It's my brother."

Her nose twitched, and she poked her face right into Mason's. For some reason, he wore a facemask with only holes for the eyes and mouth. His brother's head recoiled as his mate showed him her teeth.

Miranda snorted. Dropping her catch, she bounced—*Thump! Thump! Thump!*—back to the bed. On the way, her body melted and reshaped into that of the female he loved. And, by Ursa, naked was a good look for her, all swaying hips and bouncing boobs.

Her lips quirked as she caught the direction of his

gaze. "I caught him scrounging in our fridge. You should warn your brother that next time he touches my carrot cake, I won't just shake him like a rag doll."

Mason, who'd torn off his concealing mask, rubbed his throat. "Gee, leave for a few weeks and I come back to find you cavorting with other species. What happened to bears and woodlands creatures, even great big freaking ones, don't mix?"

Chase growled. "Watch how you speak of my mate. And turn around before I have to rip your eyes from your head. Miranda, get some clothes on."

"But then it will take more time for me to get my morning boink," she complained with a smile as she pulled on her robe.

"That's what you think."

"I'm going to keep you to that promise, honey bear."

"I've walked into the twilight zone," Mason exclaimed from where he stood staring at the wall.

"No, but you will be walking into my fist if I don't get an explanation of where the hell you've been and what you're doing sneaking into my house asking for my sweet little bunny to rip out your throat."

"I've been busy spreading the love, little brother." Mason mimed tapping some buttocks and humping, which caused Miranda to collapse into giggles as she crawled back into bed with him.

A scowl crossed his face, more because she showed more leg than he liked. He rectified that by tugging the blanket over her—he'd never shared well as a child, even with his own brother. "Sure you were, and bears hate honey. Try something a little more believable. Oh, and I met someone you might remember from your days in special ops, a croc by the name of Victor."

"Victor and his big mouth," Mason muttered.

"Spill it before I unleash my vicious rabbit and let her chase you around the place."

"Since when do you have a sense of humor?" Mason asked, incredulity in his expression. At Chase's glowering look and Miranda's snort, Mason grinned. "Fine. The short version is I was investigating the disappearances of some shifters"

"Seriously? What a coincidence. That case is the reason Chase and I met," Miranda interjected. "I'm a FUC agent. I saved my honey bear here from the mad scientist."

"As I recall, I saved your hairy ass." Chase slid a hand under the sheets and pinched said buttocks.

Miranda squealed and scooted sideways. "Ha, I just let you think you did."

"We'll talk about this later."

Miranda rolled her eyes. "Oh please, by talk you mean you're going to torture me with your evil bear lips until I concede you're right. Which, by the way, I'm fine with."

Mason watched their byplay with a jaw that kept inching downward. "Um, I hate to interrupt your lovers' tiff, but I believe I was talking about where I've been."

Chase scowled at his brother who, as Miranda kept reminding him, was ruining their morning ritual of sex followed by a shower, which usually turned into a blowjob, more sex, then breakfast. "All right, smartass. So you were investigating the same case Miranda was. How come FUC didn't know you were in on the case?"

"The higher-ups had me checking out a different angle. I was sent in to make sure the humans weren't behind it."

"And?"

"They weren't," Mason replied with a shrug.

Chase gnashed his teeth, and Miranda bounced up. "That story's boring. Get to the good part."

"What makes you think there's a good part?" Chase asked.

"Oh please. He's wearing a smug look from ear to ear and obviously cracked something or he wouldn't be here delaying my morning nookie."

"You're smarter than I would have given you credit for, long ears."

"Her name is Miranda."

"Touchy, touchy, big brother. But back to my story. I got an unexpected tip about a secret lab the military was getting experimental drugs from. Drugs that were giving their soldiers temporary, animal-like powers.

"I need some popcorn. This sounds like it would make a good movie. So, was it like some Dr. Moreau place?"

"Close. There were a lot of shifters and even more human guards. The place was insane with all kinds of state-of-the-art equipment and drugs, some of which we still don't recognize. We ended up blowing up the installation only hours before the US Marines planned to invade."

"And the person behind it all?" The mastermind whom Chase feared might still have designs on his sweet bunny.

"Dead. They holed themselves up in their office

when we arrived, and after the place blew up, we stayed long enough to make sure nothing had escaped from the inferno."

Chase let out a breath, his body relaxing. "So it's finally over. Thank Ursa."

"Ha," Miranda exclaimed, poking him in the side. "That's what you think, papa bear. There will be no relaxing for you because you are about to embark on the even more dangerous mission of parenthood."

Chase flicked his eyes from his mate to brother. "Out. Now."

"I'll be in your kitchen, eating everything but the carrot cake." With a grin and a wave, Mason left. Chase turned to his mate and pinned her to the bed.

"Are you keeping secrets from me again?"

"Who, me?" she replied with bright-eyed innocence. "Not this time. I just wanted to get rid of your brother so I could get my morning nookie."

"So you're not pregnant?"

"Not yet. But maybe if we keep trying…" She ran her hands down her body and winked.

"I should have eaten you the first time you showed up on my doorstep," he grumbled.

"Yes, you should have, but aren't you glad you didn't? Because you and I both know I am awesome."

As Chase looked upon her smiling countenance, his heart swelled. "Yes, you are. I love you, Miranda."

"And I love you too, my honey bear."

Mason yelled, his disgust clear even through the closed door. "Oh gag me!"

They did, using Mason's own socks, and then stuffed him in the hall closet. After, Chase made love to his beautiful mate, the female who'd bounced into his life and brought a spring to his step. And, for her and her alone, he even shared his honey.

****

Peering out of the hole that led to a smoldering ruin, the smallest shifter of all gnashed its tiny, pointed teeth.

Everything that could have gone wrong had, and it all started with the plot to acquire that damned bear and that even more cursed bunny.

Everything, all the hard work, the samples, the precious experiments, were now gone. Vanished in a flaming inferno set by that bloody bear's brother.

However, all was not lost. Adversity was ever a familiar friend. They'd yet to find the other hidden accounts where the bulk of the assets resided. Labs were easy to come by. Minions so simple to convince—or terrify. The progress on the computer might be lost, but the knowledge in the brain remained.

The game is not over yet.

And next time, they wouldn't see the attack coming.

Muaha—ergh—muaha—choke. Dammit!

Not quite the end...

F.U.C fun continues with Swan and the Bear.

83815738R00090

Made in the USA
Lexington, KY
15 March 2018